The Monster Menagerie

AN ANTHOLOGY FOR MONSTER LOVERS

LYONNE RILEY

Cover art by Rowan Woodcock

Cover design by Haya In Designs

Spot illustrations by Keith Montalbo

Introduction

Welcome to the Monster Menagerie!

This is an anthology of six short stories of varying lengths, following the sexy adventures of human women and their monster lovers. Some are pure steam, while others are tales of love and romance.

Read on for all tropes and content warnings for each story included in the collection.

THE MONSTER MENAGERIE

Molly works at the Monster Menagerie, a home for monsters with nowhere else to go. When she finds James the wolfman in his mating cycle, she's eager to assist, until Vargokk the resident orc gets in the way.

- M/F/M
- Why choose
- Rutting
- Light anal play
- Breeding

- Sharing is caring

DATE WITH A DINOSAUR

Remy has always been stuck in dead-end jobs until Lester, a man who merged with a dinosaur, tries to rob her at gunpoint. Little does he know that Remy has a soft spot for monsters.

- M/F
- Enemies to lovers
- Second chance romance
- Mention of drug use
- Guns and light violence

LOST IN THE SNOW

Rena is a recruiter for the Monster Menagerie, called to respond to a situation out in the field: a yeti has been stealing livestock in a remote part of Alaska, and she needs to convince him to move to the Menagerie.

- M/F
- Hurt/comfort
- Forced proximity
- Near frostbite

THE DEEP DIVE

Emma is a thrill-seeker, an adventurer. Her latest fascination? Deep-sea diving, where she comes upon a beautiful merman tied up in her tether.

- M/F
- Language barrier

- Two cocks
- Double penetration

OFFICE WEREWOLF

Raven comes to work every day with a secret vibe. It's driving Connor, a coworker who also happens to be a werewolf, absolutely mad. It's mating season and he needs to have her.

- M/F
- Rutting/mating
- Use of a sex toy at work
- Masturbation
- Transformed sex
- Cum inflation
- Knotting
- Breeding
- Pregnancy

THE LAST DRYAD

Taki the dryad is living out the rest of his shortened life at the Monster Menagerie. Ana wants more for him and offers to take him to her grandparents' cabin in the woods so he can enjoy nature again.

- M/F
- Sexy outdoor adventures
- Mid-sex transformation

The Monster Menagerie

MY JOB IS, MOSTLY, TO TAKE OUT THE TRASH.

Behind the clear plastic rooms visitors see when they come to the Menagerie, each occupant has a hidden private suite, away from prying eyes. Every private suite is accessible by a back hallway, where the doors are clearly labeled with plaques like "Isadora - Mermaid," and "Risinger - Basilisk," to tell us who lives there and what we can expect inside. Below the plaques are each occupant's rules: "Wear sunglasses," or "Bring scuba gear," or "Use a high filtration mask."

Every night during my shift, I stop at each door, equipped as required, and knock. I have to stand and wait until they answer, or in the case of the kraken in Room 106, twiddle my thumbs until he calls out that I can let myself in. I have a special key to unlock any door in the Menagerie, just for this reason.

Once I'm inside, I find their waste disposal and take each bag out to the toxic waste dumpster, then replace it with a fresh bag. Sometimes the trash reeks, like in Isadora's case, since she enjoys eating her fish as much as she enjoys leaving the guts and bones behind for me to dispose of. Other times it's normal

1

things like empty potato chip bags and used cans of E-Z Cheese.

That last item is from Arich, the demon who lives in 201. Whenever the daytime people do their ordering, Arich requests at least a few cans of cheese, which he eats in front of the guests with plain Ritz crackers. I wonder when he learned that habit during his time tormenting people in dark alleyways with promises of stealing their souls.

He doesn't have any special powers, by the way. He left Hell to venture out on his own and then realized he couldn't get back, so now he eats E-Z Cheese and works as a C++ programmer.

Four nights out of the week, I'm also tasked with bringing dinner to the creatures who call the Menagerie home. I trade off with Roger, who works the nights I'm not here. That job is easier since I can usually leave the tray on a cart at the door with each specially-prepared meal waiting under a metal cloche. Sometimes when I knock, the residents come out to fetch their food, giving me a little wave as they take the tray.

Only once did Vargokk, the orc in 300, actually take the entire cart, but I think that was just a mistake because he was hungry after his heavy workout. He loves to show off for pretty women as they walk by his exhibition room, where all occupants are asked to live at least four hours of every day so visitors of the Menagerie can gawk at them.

That's the exchange here: Allow the humans to admire you and get free room, board, and protection. Out in the real world some humans still kill monsters, and the population of many non-human species has dwindled down to almost nothing. The Gorgon is the most notable of the endangered creatures, as the last two that remain in the entire world live together in the Menagerie. Dionna and Sunitra have been married for a few hundred years at least.

Tonight is like every other night in that the Menagerie is

quiet, save for Vargokk's grunting as he bench-presses three hundred pounds again. I don't mind, because it's certainly produced results. I'm not the only human woman who takes pleasure in passing his exhibition room as he lies shirtless across his chaise lounge and reads a book. Sometimes at night, Vargokk cat-calls me as I carry another load of trash to the dumpster, and I flip him off. Once he told me that orcs had come here from another world. They passed through a portal, hoping to find help saving their dwindling civilization.

"I know I could keep a human woman very happy," he'd said, arching an eyebrow at me. "But so far, none of them will take me up on my offer."

I know he's just screwing around with me, the same way he likes to make jokes with all the other employees. He has some inside gag with Roger that involves basketball, and this always annoys me because I sort of wish my joke with Vargokk was better than fake cat-calls and hints about how good of a mom I'd be to some orc babies.

This is all very typical for the Menagerie. I've gotten accustomed to my work here, and I like the solitude of the night shift. But the one change tonight is that when I reach room 402 to take out the garbage, the door is slightly ajar.

Our residents aren't really supposed to go wandering around, though they do from time to time, and then I have to talk them into going back. They aren't prisoners here—every resident signed the papers voluntarily and chose to join the program—but they are asked to keep to their own suites, if just to minimize the potential danger of a vampire and a werewolf coming face-to-face and chewing each other to pieces.

Speaking of werewolves. According to the plaque it's James, the wolfman, who's left his door open. I knock on it and call out, "James?"

There's no answer. I lean into the door to get a look around, but the suite is dark and empty.

Overall, James is a nice guy, if reserved and a little shy. I think he's ashamed of how he looks, with pointed, furry ears high up on his head, a long wolflike muzzle, and a bushy tail. I couldn't tell you what the rest of him looks like because he always wears a collared shirt and a nice pair of slacks.

Once we talked during my smoke break, me sitting outside James's exhibition room when the park was abandoned, and he admitted that he'd been born a regular human boy until the wolf features emerged at puberty. That's when he'd learned his absent dad was one of a small handful of wolfmen left in the world. Werewolves—the kind that live in human form and then transform on the full moon—have more or less taken over their niche, leaving wolfmen to become something of legends.

"I feel like it's my responsibility to have kids," he had said, not quite looking at me. "But could I really inflict this on someone else? What if I had a son? By the time he was in high school he'd be getting bullied constantly." James had laughed a self-deprecating laugh. "Besides, who wants to mate with a wolfman? It's not like there are any wolfwomen." Another reason the wolfmen are a bizarre phenomenon—they're designed to reproduce with humans.

"You shouldn't do anything you don't want to do, especially when kids are involved," I'd said. I knew what it was like to be raised by people who regretted having you.

"The thing is that I do. I've..." His voice had trailed off, and if he wasn't furry all over, I might have seen a blush creep up his face. As it was, his yellow eyes darted away and his shoulders tightened. "I've always wanted offspring. But it's not in the cards for me."

I thought about that conversation for weeks afterwards. Sometimes, in my mind's eye, I reach out and unbuckle his belt, then unbutton the top button of his slacks and pull the zipper down. Surely James isn't as undesirable down there as he'd made it seem. Maybe, part of me thinks, I could be that person for him—that human woman he could start a family with.

There's one hitch. Even though I like James, he's a resident and I'm an employee. He's off-limits to me.

That brings me back to now and the door standing ajar with no one inside. Where has he gone? I turn down the hallway, the opposite direction from the way I came. But I don't see anything besides fluorescent lights and cheap linoleum.

"James?" I call out, and start down the hall. One of the overheads flickers, and some of my arm hairs stand on end. Where could he have gone?

Soon I reach the employee break room and that door is half-open, too. I step inside and quietly ask, "James?" Then I flick the light on.

But there's nobody here. No, instead the floor is covered in empty plastic bags of snacks, and a box of donuts is half-eaten and scattered across the counter. There's a sliver of anxiety digging into my skin as I turn around and head back out the door.

Maybe James was just hungry, like that time with Vargokk. Really, really hungry.

I head for the back door that leads out of this row and into the next one. This, too, has been left open. My footsteps slow down as I pass through it, sensing that I'm getting closer to James.

If he tore the employee lounge apart like that, what sort of mood is he in? Does the full moon affect wolfmen, too, and now he's on a rampage? I didn't register the cycle of the moon tonight. Not really on my radar of things I worry about when I'm running late for my shift.

But I've worked here for almost a year now and I've never seen James do something like this. No, he's too quiet, too normal. I don't understand it.

As I make my way down the row of rooms in the 300 hall, I

hear scratching up ahead, and then a low growling. Claws scrabble at drywall. There's a storage room here where we keep supplies, and from where I'm standing, it sounds like James is inside.

I have to talk him into going back to his room, just in case one of the other residents hears the noise and comes out to investigate. The last thing I need is a fight on my hands. So I creep closer and closer to the open door of the storage room, the growls and snarls growing louder.

"James?" I ask quietly. Suddenly, the sound stops. I peer inside the dark storage room, and a pair of yellow eyes are staring back at me through the blackness.

I can't help the little shout of alarm as I stumble backwards. The slick bottoms of my sneakers slip on the linoleum, and in a second my arms are wheeling in the air as I tumble to the floor.

Except I never land. There are a pair of soft, fuzzy arms wrapped around me, holding me up at a forty-five degree angle. When I open my eyes, James is staring down at me.

"Molly?" He helps me to a standing position again, but doesn't release me. His claws are just brushing my back, and they feel much longer and more pointed than I remember them looking before.

"What are you doing here?" I ask, my voice trembling. His yellow eyes haven't left mine.

James growls, and I wonder if I've made a mistake by disturbing him. "Hungry," he says in a strange, low tenor I haven't heard before. It's much more animal than human.

"You're hungry? But dinner was two hours ago." I know because I brought him the steak, cooked rare, with a side of rabbit, and left it at his door.

But James doesn't answer. Instead, he brings his nose down to my throat, and the wetness of it against my skin makes me gasp. He inhales sharply at the sound, and there's a warm rumble in his chest.

"Not hungry for food," he says, his claws digging just a little more into my skin. I should pull away. I should probably run and hide from whatever is going on right now, but he feels soft and yet powerful, and the scent of him is, frankly, delicious.

"Then what..." I swallow. "What are you hungry for?"

At this, James suddenly jerks back, his huge clawed hands falling away like I've burned him. He stumbles into the storage room and covers his eyes, rubbing them harshly.

"I'm sorry," he manages out, sounding much more human than before. "I'm..." He snarls in frustration as the rest of the sentence fails to leave his mouth.

"What's going on, James?" I don't like how agonized he suddenly looks. I reach out to try and steady him, to touch his bare, furry chest, but he flinches. "What's wrong?"

Finally, the words come out, but they're strained and ashamed. "I'm in my mating cycle," he says, grabbing onto the doorframe for support. "You should get away from me, Molly. As far away as you can."

Mating cycle?

Wait. This rings a bell. When I first started, I was given a list of every resident and all their warnings and triggers. I had seen something about wolfmen going through a yearly cycle where their testosterone shoots sky-high, and they want nothing more than to rut. Someone was supposed to lock him in earlier today, but they must have forgotten to look at the schedule.

Shit. Does that mean he wants to mate with me, and he's afraid he can't stop himself?

"I won't leave you here," I tell him, trying to sound as sure as I can. I have to calm him down and get him back to his room. That's the number one priority. "Come with me, James." I extend my arm to him again. Finally, after fighting a long battle with himself, he takes my offered hand in his huge clawed one, and I lead him out of the storage room. He isn't naked, but his slacks are torn, ripped open by his massive thighs and calves.

And right between his legs, a large object is stretching the pants as far as they can go while still staying on his body, thanks to his belt.

"Oh." I'm transfixed to it, this lump under his slacks. That traitorous imagination of mine is instantly imagining what it looks like under there.

"Molly!" James's voice is a harsh snarl, tinged with fear. He clenches my hand tighter inside of his. "You should leave me. Now."

"Why?" My question is so quiet I almost can't hear it myself. "What are you afraid will happen, James?"

Those bright, animal eyes narrow with frustration. "I'm afraid that I will rip off all of your clothes, right here—" he gestures at the hallway, "and fuck you until you're screaming."

Instantly my body goes blazing hot, all the way from my head to the tip of my toes. No one's said anything like that to me before. My old boyfriend, Robbie, was pretty boring in bed, one of the many reasons we broke up.

My blood is pumping hard at the idea of him shoving me up against a wall. What if I wanted that?

No. It's against the rules, not just because James isn't human, but because he's a resident, too. I could lose my job.

At the same time, he needs help. Every instinct inside of him is going wild, and locking him away in his room will just be punishment. How many years has he gone through his mating cycle and there was no one there to help him get through it?

"James," I whisper, placing a hand on his chest. His breath stills, and his lips peel back to reveal his sharp teeth. "It might be better to do that in your room, don't you think?"

"Molly...?" He grinds out the words. "Are you...?"

He can't finish his sentence, so I pull him down the hall, gesturing for him to follow me. His first step is stumbling and uncertain, but his next one is stronger, and he lets out a gust of hot breath against my neck as he understands what I'm suggesting.

But before we can make it far, his sharp claws wrap around my waist. I let out a cry of surprise as he thrusts my back hard against the wall, and his mouth descends on my neck. At first I think he's going to attack me, tear out the soft chords inside my throat and drink his fill of my blood. But instead he runs his fangs over my skin, never once breaking the surface, his hot breath sending sharp bursts of need into my veins.

"Oh, James," I groan, as his long tongue laps at the place where my neck and collarbone meet. That enormous lump under his pants is pressing at my abdomen. I need to free it. While he licks me, I reach out to unbuckle his belt and then open the top button of his pants, just like in my fantasy. He goes rigid, his tongue stilling. Before I've even made it to the zipper, his cock slides free of the band and he lets out a low snarl.

I push the pants down and my eyes drop to his waist, taking in all of him. His cock is pink and glistening with moisture, and there's a big lump around the base I've never seen before. I wonder what it does. Even though it's strange, my hands know right where to go, and soon I have both of them wrapped around his shaft. It's so large my fingers won't go all the way around.

"Fuck," he growls, and his claws dig into the cheap drywall behind me. There's already come dripping from the indentation on his cockhead, sliding down in white rivulets toward my palms. As l use it to lubricate my hands, there's a pulsing energy between my legs. I stroke him up and down, and he snarls and licks my throat again, then drags his tongue to my ear. His claw reaches up, and I stop breathing as it settles on my collar. Then he slashes down and my shirt rips open, and I let out a cry of surprise as he draws the tear all the way down to my belly button, leaving the shirt in two halves.

I'm suddenly revealed, and I can't believe we're doing this, right here in the hallway. It's almost as hot as the fact I'm about to get ravaged by James the Wolfman.

"What's going on out here?" A door flies open, and the doorknob slams into the wall. I jolt with surprise, but James doesn't move. We both look over to find Vargokk, dressed in only his gym shorts, staring back at us. I know exactly what this looks like.

"What the fuck are you doing to her?" the orc demands, his lips curling with rage and drawing his tusks high up past his nose. Before I can speak, he lunges at us, ready to tear James open.

"Wait! Vargokk, stop!" I manage to wriggle out of James's grip, and plant myself between them.

Vargokk tries to put on the brakes. He shouts, "Molly!" but slams into me anyway. He smells like sweat, and the heavy musk of it is everywhere as he gets his arms around me, yanking me hard against his chest. He staggers a few steps back, removing me from James's clutches.

"No!" James roars. "Mine!" This interruption has triggered his animal fury, and his claws are all pointed at Vargokk, ready to fight to get me back.

"Vargokk, it's fine!" I struggle against his huge, sculpted chest. "Put me down!"

"What do you mean, 'it's fine'?!" He's aghast. "It's very not fine! That wolf was about to—"

"Did you see the part where I had my hands on his cock or not?" I'm really annoyed now. Vargokk is backing away, still holding me tight, as James advances on us. The wolfman's yellow eyes have lost all trace of humanity, and his fangs are dripping with drool.

"Molly..." Vargokk brings his mouth down so he can speak into my ear. "You were going to fuck him?"

I nod furiously. "Before you interrupted."

The orc hisses in irritation. But almost immediately, something hard and firm jumps against my lower back. "You must be crazy, Molly." Vargokk's grip tightens. "It isn't safe. He's..."

I wriggle against his arms, which only earns another jump from whatever is pressed into my ass. I think I have a pretty good idea. "And who are you to tell me what I can and can't do?"

James roars again. "Mine!" He reaches out to me, claws bared, and Vargokk still doesn't let me go.

"Well, I... Uh..." We've backed up so far that we've finally reached Vargokk's open door. "I just thought that, you know, if you were going to do that with any of us, it would be with, um..." His voice drops to a whisper. "Well, me."

So Vargokk hasn't just been kidding around with me all this time.

"What?" My breath is coming heavier. "Why didn't you say anything sooner?"

"We don't have time to be arguing about this," Vargokk snaps. "Tell your wolf friend you're not interested."

"It's not going to help! He's in his mating cycle—he *needs* to do this, or he won't stop."

Vargokk groans. "Of course."

James, consumed by his feral need, is almost on top of us. "Mine." He reaches out to me again, and his cock is even bigger, more swollen than before. Despite Vargokk's interference, my need for it has grown immense. But I can't possibly let him fuck me now, in this hallway, right in front of another resident of the Menagerie. Especially not one who just told me he's been nursing a crush on me for who knows how long.

Suddenly, behind me, Vargokk lets me go. He grabs one of James's huge wrists in his hand, and yanks the wolfman towards him. James lets out a yelp of surprise.

"Hey, buddy," Vargokk snarls, and uses his other hand to smack James right across the muzzle. "Snap out of it. You're going to hurt somebody like that."

Oh, shit. That's how you get your throat torn out by a rutting wolfman.

But to my surprise, James's eyes do regain some of their humanity again. He squints at me, then at Vargokk, and then down at his exposed, dripping cock.

"Fuck," he growls.

"Yeah," Vargokk agrees. The orc glances over at where I'm pinned against the doorframe between them, and takes in my exposed chest. His gym shorts are much less restrictive than James's pants were, easily hinting at the shape of him underneath it. How can he possibly be hard for this? "You weren't really going to take all that, were you, Molly?" the orc asks, nodding at James's enormous cock.

I feel my entire face go bright red. "Well, that was the plan."

"I... I need to leave," James mutters, trying to back away from us. "I shouldn't... I can't ..."

I'm going to lose my chance. Now that I'm here, now that I've touched him, I want to feel him. I also can't let him run away and possibly escape the Menagerie. Who knows what kind of damage he could do out there in the wider world?

"Hey, James." I approach him like I would a frightened animal, and bring my hand back to his cock. He groans as I stroke it gently. "You don't need to go." I glance over my shoulder at Vargokk. "Right? He should stay here, where we can keep an eye on him."

The orc seems to understand my message, much to his dismay. We are standing right in his doorway, after all—his private suite is the perfect place to lock in an extremely horny, somewhat dangerous wolfman.

"He's going to fuck you like a dog," Vargokk says, eyeing me. Then one side of his mouth curls up, his tusk almost reaching his eye. "But that's what you want, isn't it? You want to have all his little puppies, don't you?"

"I never said *that*." That doesn't mean I hadn't thought it, though.

"Hmm." And yet he still has a ghost of a smile on his face. "Fine. Everyone get inside." Vargokk hauls James in through the door by one arm, then I follow and close the door behind me with a *slam*.

Vargokk's apartment is clean and minimalist, and smells a little like air freshener. My eyes have strayed from the panting wolfman with the drooling cock over to the orc, who stands there shirtless, an enormous boner tenting his gym shorts.

"What's that about?" I ask, pointing at it.

His face darkens, and I think it's the orc version of blushing. "You're not wearing a shirt, Molly."

I glance down. "Oh. Right." James's eyes are equally fixated on my chest. "Sorry."

"I'm not." Vargokk moves towards me and James lets out an instinctual growl. "What?" the orc flips him off. "I can't appreciate, too?"

James rivets his golden eyes on me like I'm the only person in the room. "If I don't get my hands on you soon," he manages between gritted teeth, "I won't be able to stay in control. The wolf will take over again."

His cycle is in full swing, and we were interrupted in the middle of fulfilling it. But now we have an extra complication, one that's as toned as a bodybuilder, with muscles I've never even seen on a human before. Vargokk arches an eyebrow as I study him, and his cock jumps again under his shorts.

"See, James?" He slaps the wolfman on the back. "You're not the only one with a dying species. And I think Molly is just as interested in me as she is in you." He read me dead to rights. I've wanted to climb Vargokk like a tree since I started working here, but he's always been full of himself, and I've always been sure he was just trying to get my goat by hitting on me.

Hair bristles on the back of James's neck and his tail puffs out, like he's ready to fight Vargokk then and there—just what I was trying to avoid.

"Hey," I murmur, running a hand down his chest to his cock. "I'm staying right here." James leans hard into my palm and immediately his shoulders relax. "There we go." Vargokk's eyes are so wide they're nearly round. He's gotten even harder, as if watching us is doing it for him.

"This isn't fair at all," he grumbles, dragging one hand up along the shaft hidden inside his shorts. His eyes don't leave mine as he lets out a ragged breath.

That's when I have the most dastardly wicked idea I've ever had in my life.

"Then come over here," I say. I hold out a hand to him, and Vargokk frowns at it suspiciously. "I have two arms."

"You've got to be kidding." At first I'm certain he's going to turn me down without question. But as his eyes travel from my chest to where my hand is wrapped around James's cock, his expression changes to something much more mischievous. He takes a step towards us, then another step. Utterly oblivious to anything else, James licks me just under my jawline while I continue stroking him. Once Vargokk is close enough, I reach down the front of his gym shorts with my free hand and drag my fingers along the hard seam on the underside of his shaft. His cock is huge and throbbing and standing straight up for me. Before I can free it from its prison, Vargokk reaches around behind me and rips the back of my bra right out of the way.

"Hey!" It tumbles to the floor. "That one was my favorite."

"I'll buy you a new one," Vargokk says gruffly. I guess I'll take it, since I'm pretty sure he makes a decent salary working remotely. Before I can blink, his hands descend to my breasts. His palms are calloused from lifting, and his fingers are firm and eager. When I gasp, James seems to finally realize what's going on—literally right under his nose—and lets out a low, possessive snarl.

"You'll get your attention," I tell him, kissing his wet nose. James snuffs and licks the edges of my lips, then nips them until they part and slides his tongue in. I imagine what other sensitive place on my body might also part for him this way.

Vargokk plucks at each of my nipples, my head twisted now so James can get access to my mouth while the orc has his way down below. Every last inch of me has grown hyper-sensitive, and the twist of Vargokk's fingers and the invasion of James's tongue at the same time feels exquisite. I finally get the orc's shorts off his hips, and his cock leaps to attention. When I get my hand around it, he lets out a guttural groan.

"I need you," James whispers into my ear. More of his come is dripping down his cock into my palm. I rub it all over the head, squeezing him. "I need to be inside of you, *now*."

His commanding tone takes me by surprise, and my lower lips fill with hot blood. I want that, too. I've been wanting it since he first told me what he told me what he was going to do to me.

"Now, now," Vargokk says, privy to every word of our conversation. "Who said you could go first, dog?"

James snarls. "That was the plan before you came along."

With a thoughtful *hmm*, Vargokk's hand drifts down over my belly button to the top of my jeans. He slides his hand over them and down between my legs, and unconsciously, my hips buck into his palm.

"You would just shove yourself right in there?" Vargokk asks in a thick, velvety tone. "Without paying her the proper attention first?"

This time when James growls, it's weaker, like he knows the orc has a point. Vargokk lets out a chuckle and unbuttons my pants. "Miss Molly?" His eyes, which are orange-yellow all the way through the sclera, are twinkling. "May I? I won't be a brute like *some*."

He wants to get into my pants? Well, twist my arm.

"Yes," I whisper.

Once the button is undone and the zipper pulled down, just my underwear are left. They're nothing spectacular, but I wasn't really preparing for a threesome tonight.

Up above me, James sucks in a deep breath, and his ears press back in pleasure. "You smell so good," he groans, burying his nose in my hair. "I can detect how aroused you are from here."

That sounds like a bad thing, but the way the wolfman's strangely-pointed cock is now urgently poking at my hip, I think he likes it. Vargokk's thick, sturdy fingers trace over the edges of my underwear, dipping between my legs to rub my clit through the fabric.

"You're so wet for us," Vargokk says as his hand finally dips inside. He lets out a groan when he finds how much my juices have already pooled there. He slips through my folds, searching out my delicate nub. I moan and wriggle as James plays with my nipples, and the pads of Vargokk's fingers brush gently over my clit. I'm dripping into his palm.

"I want to taste you," snarls James, his nostrils flaring wildly. "I need to."

Gently, I push both of them away, and my eyes are blessed with a feast. Below his fiercely muscled hips, Vargokk's huge, powerful green cock is pointed up, ready to spear me through. James has muscle, too, hidden under his soft, brown pelt. From the fur at James's groin, his own wet member protrudes straight out towards me, and I can't help wondering what each of them will feel like.

I want James's incredible, long tongue on me, like he promised. And right now, my mouth feels rather empty without him kissing me. Imagining what I want, I kneel down on the floor, and gesture for James to come towards me. He obeys, drool glistening on his teeth, and his lips curl back in hunger. He shoves me down the rest of the way to the carpet, claws pinning me to the floor. Without much ado he traverses down my belly to the patch of hair at the base of my pelvis, where he snuffles it and groans.

"The smell of you..." He inhales heavily. "Nothing like it."

He doesn't have to open my legs because my thighs fall apart for him of their own accord. Vargokk is watching, cock harder than ever, and I crave nothing more than to touch it. As if he can read my mind, he joins us on the floor. I don't take him in my hands right away—no, I start by exploring down to the huge sac that hangs between his legs. The skin is soft here, and his testicles are full to bursting.

"Ah!" The sudden wet heat of James's tongue tears my attention away. I grip Vargokk's balls hard and he grunts, a hand tangling in my hair. Remembering what I was doing before, I wrap both hands around the orc's immense shaft and stroke him, hard. His hips thrust into me, and he groans out my name.

James's mouth is flawless, his tongue racing up and down my lower lips, tasting my soft entrance and then sliding back up again to twist and dance around my clit. Nothing has ever felt like this. Before I'm sure what's happening, I'm riding upward on a wave of James's wet tongue and crashing down over the rocks. I moan and twitch while he laps all of me up, and a growl of pleasure rumbles in his throat.

But having my hands around Vargokk's cock isn't all I want. I need to wrap my mouth around it, to taste him the way that James is tasting me. I clamber up onto my hands and knees, and James dutifully follows. With my ass raised in the air, I lick Vargokk's wide crown.

"Oh?" he asks, running a hand through my hair. "Is that so?"

I kiss the head of his cock as if to say, *that is so*.

James now crouches behind me with his snout buried in my pussy, apparently not to be deterred from licking me silly. This time he plunges inside my slit with his tongue, and I moan into Vargokk's cock.

"Oh, damn," he grunts, sliding it deeper into my mouth. "That's incredible, Molly."

Behind me James rubs one claw gently over my clit while he fits all of his tongue inside of me, widening me, preparing me. Suddenly the tongue isn't enough—it's not filling me the way I desperately need.

"Please," I whimper around Vargokk's cock. "I want you, James. Please."

Vargokk grumbles. "It won't work," he tells the wolfman. "You can fill her up all you like, but it will be my seed that wins." Just the idea of this massive, dark green cock inside me while I'm already full with James's come makes my entire body spasm. It will be the filthiest thing I've done in my life, and my heated blood is ready for it.

"Wrong," James responds, continuing to torment my sensitive nub while he brings himself into position behind me. "I'm first. She will have *my* pups."

Well, that was already what I'd wanted, long before I found James's door hanging open tonight.

"Stop arguing," I chide them. "What happens, happens."

While James kneels behind me, I suck on Vargokk's cock even harder. I've never been so ready. Suddenly I feel James slide between my thighs, slicking his cockhead over my clit, again and again. He's already dripping for me.

"Please!" I moan the words through the cock in my mouth. Vargokk shudders underneath me.

"Mine," James growls back, and drags himself back up to prod at my slit. I feel my lips gently part for him, and I wonder what foolishness overtook me to welcome a cock of that size inside me at *this* angle. Doggy-style is about as intense as it gets for me. I'm not immune to the irony.

James slides in deeper and immediately, my tight channel

constricts around him, preventing him from entering even further.

"Slow," I whimper.

Behind me James is gasping for air, his claws sinking into the flesh of my ass. I can sense he's trying with everything he has not to simply ram into me up to the hilt.

"Should have taken me first," Vargokk chuckles. "It's not too late."

"But..." We were so close. I almost had James inside me, right where I need him—even though I know Vargokk's right, and it'll be uncomfortable to take so much so fast.

"I can't control it," James growls, panting heavily as he sits back on his heels. "I will hurt her."

With a smug snort, Vargokk withdraws his cock from my mouth. "It's a good thing I'm here," he says. "Stand back, wolf. Let someone with a sound mind take over."

James moves into my field of vision and crouches on his haunches, bringing one clawed hand up to stroke himself.

"Now Molly," Vargokk says, gently turning me over so I'm lying on my back, breasts and pussy exposed to the air. I'm shuddering, twitching with anticipation. "I'm going to warm you up right, if you'll have it." He's kneeling in front of me, his abdominals carved into sharp lines that wind down his front and curl around his cock. His muscles ripple as he draws his finger down between my legs.

"Yes." My voice comes out a pathetic whine, but it's because I need him. He's bigger than any man I've ever seen before, cock pointed up to the heavens and glistening with pre-come. James's eyes are focused on us intently as he strokes himself harder, faster.

"Good," Vargokk says, one of his tusks nearly reaching his eyes as he gives me a sideways smile. He dips a finger inside me, just briefly, and moves it around in a gentle circle, helping my tight channel relax for him. Then he puts in another finger and my head falls back, right underneath James's incredible cock. I can't help but lick it while he strokes himself, tasting the musky, salty fluid dripping from the tip. Vargokk's fingers speed up, curling to brush against the inside of me, while his thumb finds its way to my clit. Somehow, he manages to tease that at the same time as he finger-fucks me, and I'm already so close to toppling into the abyss again.

That's when I feel Vargokk remove his fingers, and something else even warmer, even rounder and thicker, takes their place. I lift my head to find a sly smile on the orc's face as he guides himself through my swollen, slick folds, then pauses to continue thumbing my clit. I've never felt anything like this before, and I want nothing else than for him to slip the rest of the way inside me. Now I'm licking the underside of James's cock frantically while my hands stroke him, one around his shaft and the other teasing the sac between his legs. He groans heavily, panting, eyes glued to where Vargokk is pushing his way inside me. I'm widening for him, opening for him, my body spreading apart to allow him in. Only then does he sink another inch deeper, and the moan I let out doesn't even sound like me. His thumb never stops stroking my clit, and before he's even halfway to his destination, I'm starting to clench and throb.

"Agh," Vargokk grunts, pausing his invasion to gather himself. "You're so tight, I'm not sure if you can take all of me."

I run my hands even faster up and down James's cock, and he lets out a hard grunt.

"I can," I say. "I can. Please."

The orc's grin is absolutely feral. He clutches my hips, fingers buried in my flesh, and sinks the rest of the way in. I cry out this time as Vargokk finds his place deep down, cockhead settling into where it belongs. "Oh, the feel of you," he growls, reaching out to take my nipple and pinch it. He rolls it around in his fingers as he slowly pulls his cock free of my vice. James is snarling, more come dribbling out of him. I lick it all off, then suck him hard.

At the perfect moment, Vargokk slides back into me. I can feel his blood pulsing as he finds his seat once more and there he rocks back and forth, just reveling in the sensation of fully filling me up. It's so beautifully, painfully, wonderfully slow that I feel like I might burst if he doesn't give me more. He looks cool and collected, but I can tell by the way his movements are speeding up that he's coming close to the edge. And yet, he wants me to go over first. The heady scent of James's come, the sensation of Vargokk's cock slicking in and out of me with wet slaps is enough to drive me straight over the side of the cliff. A cry tears itself from my throat as I clamp down hard, and Vargokk lets out a harsh grunt. He thrusts harder, faster, and soon, he's swelling up huge inside me. I'm so tight I can barely take him, and this extra girth draws out my climax even further. I'm on a rollercoaster hurtling down from the sky.

"Ah, fuck!" Vargokk shoves himself inside me as deep as he can, gritting his teeth as he unloads everything. Immediately his hot come drips down my ass onto the floor, and I don't think I've ever felt something more erotic. Over my head, James is panting hard, having watched the entire thing with a heated fascination.

I lie there, gasping for air, as Vargokk's comforting fingers splay across my belly. He *hmms* with pleasure. "You'll grow a very strong orc in here," he whispers, just for me. My whole body twitches at the thought of it. "Now," Vargokk says in a deep, authoritative voice, "I want you to get on your knees, Molly. I want to watch you take the dog's cock as deep as you can."

My gaze darts to him in surprise, and his satisfied expression has morphed into a wicked smile. There's an obscene, wet *pop!* as Vargokk withdraws himself from me, and now his green cock is hanging down between his legs, dripping with our juices.

James snarls with anticipation, and I know I can take him now. I manage to turn myself over with James's eager assistance. His cock is a very different shape from Vargokk's, with a less defined head, and a more pronounced, pointed tip. It's thicker all the way from head to base, where that strange lump resides. I wonder what he's going to do with it. There's no way it could fit inside me, right?

Once I'm on my knees, James crouches down behind me, and where I expected to feel that soft, wet cock, his tongue appears instead. He licks up everything, my come and Vargokk's, and then lets out a rough groan as he swallows it. But that's not all—no, he traces his tongue upward, away from my soft, throbbing pussy to the puckered place between my cheeks.

"Oh my god," I say, recoiling a little. But James chases me, and I find I'm whimpering as his long, skillful tongue circles my tiny hole, gently prying it open. I've never had anyone there before, and the sensation of it is foreign, surprising, and delightful. He presses his tongue in, circling the edges of me, and I'm overcome. Vargokk chuckles, and when I look up, he's already stroking himself again while he watches us.

All this exploration has made me need James's cock even more. "Please," I whisper. "I'm so empty."

"I will fix that," comes his guttural reply. His tongue withdraws, and that's when I can feel the firm, pointed tip of him already slipping inside my pussy where I've been thoroughly softened and prepared. I can't help a cry as he shoves himself deep on his first thrust, and James roars in victory. He's even thicker than Vargokk while somehow also softer, and the pointed tip of him drags along the inside of my walls. I've never felt anything like it, and I have to bite down on my arm to keep in my scream.

The orc is getting hard again as his huge hands stroke up

and down his slick cock. He kneels by my hips, where James is fucking me hard and fast, each thrust running that soft tip against my sensitive insides. I'm so overwhelmed by the feel of him that there are tears in my eyes.

That's when I feel Vargokk's finger working against my ass where James has already gotten me wet and prepared. I do scream this time when he slides it in. With his other hand he continues stroking himself, all while James rams me over and over again.

I'm not sure I can take any more. The pressure of Vargokk's finger filling me against the wolfman's enormous cock is more than my body can bear. I'm nothing but white-hot nerve endings, every one of them firing spark after spark as the two of them fuck me. I bury my face in the crook of my elbow and manage out the words, "I'm going to come."

"Good," James snarls. "Come all over me."

His command drags me closer to the bottomless pit, where the thrusts of Vargokk's finger sends me careening into the emptiness. I'm flying and falling and spinning, but James never stops plundering me, even when I'm so tight that he struggles to shove himself back in.

Finally, Vargokk withdraws his hand, and I gasp with relief and emptiness. He just chuckles. "I'm not done with you," he murmurs, and positions himself in front of me so his drooling, dark green cock sits right in front of my mouth.

I'm more than happy to bring it between my lips, and he groans in abject pleasure. He tastes like both of us, and I take him as deep into my throat as I can while James picks up his pace behind me. We're so slippery and I'm so tight that every one of the wolfman's strokes makes a smacking noise. His groans escalate, and that's when I feel the lump at the base of his cock starting to worm its way inside me.

There's no way. There's just no way.

"I saw that neat little feature," Vargokk says as his hips

thrust against my mouth. "I hope you can take it." I hope that, too. But James's furious fucking has loosened me up so much that somehow, it manages to fit, and I can't help but scream against Vargokk's cock, which muffles me.

James leans down, his hand dipping between my legs so his claw can brush against my clit. His other hand runs up my spine and into my hair, where he brings my ear up to his lips. "I'm going to stuff you so full of my seed," he growls, lapping at my earlobe with his long tongue, "that you'll be full of my pups."

Vargokk snorts, and I can feel his cock starting to thicken up inside my mouth. "You can dream, dog."

With a snarl, James slides in deeper than ever. Not only is he preparing to unleash, but the lump at the base of him is swelling up thick and fat, too. With his claw brushing over my clit over and over, I sob around Vargokk, who has filled my mouth and throat as far as they can go.

I've never climaxed like this. It feels as if a crack has appeared in the world and it's crashing down on top of me. My pussy is sucking James in deep and he's roaring behind me, slamming through my orgasm and stretching it out, further and further.

"Molly," I hear him snarl. "I hope you're ready." I don't know what he means, but I want anything he gives me.

Suddenly, he's stuck, deep inside me. His lump has swelled up so much that my tight hole won't let it come out again, and there, James unleashes. He's pumping so much seed into me that my channel fills all the way to the brim, and I cry out as my body stretches to accommodate. I'm sucking on Vargokk's cock so hard, my brain firing agonizing pleasure into every corner of my body, that he's reaching his climax, too. He groans and buries himself deep in my throat, and hot come spills out of my lips.

I'm breathing so hard that my gasps are sticking together. I collapse to the floor, but James is still trapped inside me, thick and full and hard. A hand gently brushes through my hair, and I look up to find Vargokk staring down at me with a warm affection in his eyes.

"You'll be all right," he tells me, fingers sliding down to cup my cheek. "I've heard some baser creatures can do this."

James falls down on top of me, his snout pressed into my back. "Sorry," he grunts. "It'll just take a few minutes for it to come down." I have so many questions, but my brain is too overloaded to ask any of them. "It's just meant to keep my seed inside you as long as possible."

But Vargokk doesn't look concerned. "Your little trick won't help you win."

"We'll see." James nuzzles the back of my head. "Thank you, Molly. That was everything."

It really and truly was.

As promised, James's massive knot does eventually soften, and he's able to slide out of me. Come rushes down my thighs, and I fall flat on the floor on my belly. While Vargokk lifts me gently into his lap, James gets up and returns a moment later with a dish towel, which he wets with his tongue and uses to clean me up. I can barely move, but that doesn't seem to be a problem with these two around. Vargokk picks me up into his arms and carries me into his bedroom, which is surprisingly well-decorated. James climbs into the bed first, and reaches out to take me as the orc follows suit. Together they slide me under the blankets, and I'm so warm and fuzzy all over that my eyes close on their own.

On one side, James leans his wet nose against my neck, and on the other side, Vargokk tangles up his leg with mine. Here, I know that I'm safe and treasured. Here, nothing can touch me, except my powerful orc and my wild wolfman.

Hopefully I won't get in trouble in the morning—but if I do, this was totally worth it.

Date with a Dinosaur

WHEN THE ASTEROID ENTERED OUR SOLAR SYSTEM HEADED straight for Earth, we thought that surely we would all die.

Sometimes I'm not sure if what actually happened was worse. The asteroid hit and destroyed a few towns on the eastern seaboard, but the biggest catastrophe wasn't the strike itself, all the people lost to it, or even the fallout. It was what the asteroid did *after* it landed.

To this day, it seems random who was affected by the asteroid and who wasn't. I was spared and so were my parents. One of my cousins, though, didn't get so lucky. She works at a turkey processing plant in Idaho, and after the asteroid did its thing... well, she isn't so human anymore. Now she has a beak and a wattle and wings for arms, complete with feathers. She's just one of billions of people who were irrevocably changed by the asteroid. Nothing on planet Earth will ever be the same again.

Now, though, enough time has passed that everyone has grown accustomed to seeing their former friends and colleagues deeply changed. My dad's boss is a deer-man now because he was out hunting when the asteroid smashed into

Earth. He has big antlers that hit the doorframe whenever he enters or leaves his office, and dainty little hooves.

"At least I don't need to wear shoes anymore," Dad's boss said. He also isn't much of a meat-eater now.

The asteroid didn't change anything for me. I had no life plan before it, and I still don't now. I've hopped from dead-end job to dead-end job for years. Out of high school I was a waitress at an iHop, then I became a night concierge at a hotel until I fell asleep on the job and got fired. I'm just really good at screwing up, as it turns out. I had an admin assistant gig for a small construction office, but I routed a big, important business call to my mother's house by accident and that was enough to get rid of me in the first round of layoffs.

Swipe. Ding. Swipe. Ding. Another box of cigarettes, another Snickers bar, another twenty dollars on the pump, please. Working at a gas station convenience store is lower than I ever thought I'd drop, but the pay is decent and the hours are just what I like: I start in the afternoon and work through the night when the fewest number of people are coming through. It leaves me alone most of the time to read magazines off the shelf or play Candy Crush on my phone.

While I'm playing, I think about how my cousin can't use a smart phone anymore thanks to her stupid wings. I wonder how she's getting along and think about calling to check in, until I remember—right, the wings. Maybe she has a bluetooth thing figured out now.

I'm swiping a customer's card and handing it back to her, trying not to get my hand clipped by her sharp cat's claws, when a hooded figure steps inside the gas station. People in hoods aren't necessarily suspicious, but it's the stiff hunch of the shoulders and the hands buried inside the front pouch pocket that rings an alarm bell in my mind. Whoever it is, they're anxious, and what would they be anxious about in a convenience store unless they were tripping on acid or about to rob me blind?

I finish up the housecat woman's transaction, keeping my eyes on the hooded figure as he starts browsing the aisles. A huge green tail sprouts from underneath his hoodie, thick, long and scaly with dark, bumpy ridges winding their way up the spine. He's one of the Affected, clearly, though I wonder what creature he merged with to wind up with a tail like that one. His feet are hidden inside heavy combat boots covered in buckles, and the tromp of his soles follows him around the store.

Maybe I'm jumping to conclusions, because he only seems interested in the sunflower seeds. It's hard not to be suspicious when you're a mid-twenties woman working late nights alone, but I have to give people the benefit of the doubt. So I pull out my phone and start browsing Instagram, waiting until he's found whatever midnight munchie he's looking for.

"Put your hands up."

The voice is deep and commanding. When I look up, there's the pitch black barrel of a gun pointed right at my face.

God damn it. My instincts are always right.

Behind the gun, the hooded man has deep-inset eyes that are completely yellow with no sclera. His snout is rounded with two flared nostrils at the tip, and his fangs are bared. Underneath he wears a black, spiked collar, and the hand he's holding out with the gun is similarly wrapped in studded leather.

He must have merged with some kind of lizard in the incident. That's the only way to explain the clawed hand that flicks the safety off the gun.

"Hey, hey," I say, holding up my hands in surrender. "There's no need, man."

The lizard guy tilts his head to one side. "Are you going to give me the cash in the register, or what?"

I sigh and roll my eyes. "Come on, have you ever worked in

one of these places? I can't open the register unless there's a transaction. I'm not the manager or anything."

"That's bullshit," he says. A piercing in his right nostril jangles as he inhales a sharp breath. "I've seen this in movies a dozen times."

"Real life isn't a movie," I say. "If you want this register to open, you're going to have to buy something."

Grumbling, the lizard seems to accept that I'm telling the truth, and he drops his eyes to start browsing the candy selection below the counter. While he's distracted I try to think: How can I get out of this alive with my job intact? If he robs me, I'm definitely going to get fired—I've been on thin ice with this boss for a while. I can't get booted out on my ass again.

While my assailant is trying to decide between white and milk chocolate Reese's, I take a deep, steadying breath. Courage has never been my biggest strength, but my fear of being unemployed is powerful, so I reach out to snatch the gun from his hand.

"What the fuck?" Though I've managed to get my fingers around the barrel and push it away from my face, the lizard still has control. His glare is scathing as he tries to yank the gun out of my grasp, and the barrel swings to one side and then the other when I don't let go. I hope to god he doesn't accidentally shoot me.

"Are you crazy?" He steps back and pulls with all his might —which only drags me up and over the counter since I'm not about to let go of that gun.

"You're the one trying to rob me! Who's the crazy one here?" I manage to sound flippant even though my heart is pounding like a drum circle in my ears.

"Let go!" Now I'm on top of the counter, and I have a firmer grip on the gun than I did before. His hands are big and bulky, and he seems to have a harder time holding onto the metal with his slick scales than I do with my soft, squishy skin. The lizard's hoodie has fallen off, revealing the high, spiked ridges that run all the way up his back and end between his eyes. With the piercings in his eyebrow and his ridges, he's actually kind of cute.

"I'm not letting go, so either you drop it, or—" I'm cut off when he finally drags me all the way over the counter, sending me crashing into him. As we tumble to the floor the gun goes flying across the convenience store, skittering on the cheap linoleum.

My attacker is now underneath me, and his muscles are so dense he didn't do much to cushion my fall. Now I've had the breath knocked right out of me. Gasping and aching, I reach for the gun, but the lizard is stronger than I am. With a deft heave he pushes me off, and his significantly longer arm starts fishing for the gun. What he doesn't know is that I'm much more desperate than he is, so I'm quicker to rise to my feet. I make a point of stepping on his arm as I pass, and he roars in pain—a sound that is definitively inhuman.

Then the gun is in my quivering hands, the barrel trained on the lizard in the hoodie. He starts to stand up.

"Stay where you are!" Even I can see the wobble of the gun. I've never held one before, and I definitely don't know how to use it. Sure, you can push the trigger, but what then? I can't kill someone, especially this handsome lizard with a choke collar. Maybe I'd get a self-defense pass in the eyes of the law, but that would never allay my guilt.

His bright yellow eyes seem to understand all of this in that split second, because he spins like a top and takes off out the door at a run.

Damn it. I should let him go and figure out later what to do with the gun. I could call the cops right away and explain what happened, but I'd have no video to back me up. The camera with the red blinking light is fake, designed to ward off petty thieves like this one without costing my cheap boss and a few extra bucks.

No, this bastard tried to rob me. I'm going to force him to apologize, and then I'm going to turn him in. Maybe there'll be some reward money in it for me. So I press the button under the counter to call the police and then take off after him.

Those heavy combat boots won't get him very far—not at a good clip, at least. Unluckily for him I'm in my sneakers, thanks to the fact I have to stand up all day at work, and I weave through the gas pumps after his retreating shape.

"Stop!" I yell out, waving the gun over my head. He doesn't listen, of course, and races across the street toward the trees. We're on the edge of town, but I know these woods well because I usually come to smoke weed here on my break. Fine. If he's going to make this into a chase, I'll give him a chase.

Even though I've lost sight of him through the trees, I can easily hear his heavy boots crunching twigs and pine needles up ahead. I pick up my pace, my lungs fighting the whole way as I crash through the brush. What he doesn't know? There's a drop-off coming up ahead that heads down into a deep ravine. That's Oregon, for you—you can't tell when there's going to be a big ravine.

"You're going to fall if you're not careful," I shout after him.

"Piss off!" he shouts back.

Great, that makes it easy to hone in on his location. I power on ahead in the direction of his voice. Then I hear a shriek, and the cracking of branches as he starts his tumble down the steep hill. Just as I reach the edge and come to a stop, the sound of crashing halts and a deep, pained groaning follows.

"Told you," I call down to him. The lizard guy just groans again, deeper and more pained this time, and now I'm worried those cops are going to come and find a body.

There's only one thing I can do. I drop the gun at the base of a tree and lower myself over the side of the ravine, holding onto a thick root. Rappelling down makes me wonder how on earth I plan to get back up again, but now I'm halfway there and I don't have a choice but to keep going. Ferns whip at my face as my hand slips, and when I grapple at the hillside to stop my fall, my fingers come away empty and covered in mud.

Great.

With one misstep I start to slide down the hill myself, but I have less far to go. Each bump knocks the wind out of me, and when I finally come to a stop, I'm halfway into a blackberry bush, the thorns pricking me like I'm a pincushion.

"God damn it," I grumble, extracting myself from the bush and leaving gashes in my shirt and jeans.

The lizard guy lies nearby in a wet divot in the ground, struggling to get up. "Why are you *chasing* me?" He has to gasp to get the words out.

"You're the one who put a gun in my face," I say, finally righting myself. "I deserve an apology for that."

His big mouth falls open, revealing two rows of sharp teeth. "You've got to be kidding." He tries again to sit up, but he groans in pain and clutches his side. "I think I broke a rib or something, and it's just because you wanted an *apology*?"

Standing over him like this, I can get a better view of his anatomy. He has textured ridges for eyebrows, and two rings in the left one. I think it's a tattoo on his neck peeking out from under his hoodie. His body is huge and muscular, and I'm not sure how I managed to knock him down. Gosh. For a guy who got merged with a lizard by the asteroid, he's pretty hot, even though now he's covered in mud.

I crouch next to him and hold out my arm. "Here, take my hand. I'll help you up."

"What?" He pushes me away. "Piss off. I've got this." He tries again to stand up, but he can't get his legs under him. I grab him by the bicep and pull. Finally choosing to lean against me, he manages to get to his feet.

He pushes me off as soon as he's upright, and falls back to lean against a tree. "You're fucking crazy," he says, gasping and clutching his side.

"That's what everyone tells me." I gesture at his injury. "Can I look?" I need him to be fine. He could easily tell the cops I pushed him into the ravine, and then I'd be under scrutiny, too.

He growls like he's going to object, but now that we're standing in front of each other he's frozen, his eyes roving up my body until they land on my face. His lip curls on one side, revealing more teeth.

"Fine." He holds his arm away from his injured ribcage. "Go ahead, look. As if that will help anything."

When I bring my hand up to test his side, I'm surprised that he's rather warm. "I thought lizards were cold-blooded," I say, pressing down slightly on his rib. My dad is a nurse, and I've nearly broken my ribs enough times to know what to look for. The lizard guy grunts, but doesn't push me off.

"I'm not a *lizard*," he says between gritted teeth. "I'm a *dinosaur*. Well, partly dinosaur—an Allosaurus. You know."

I test another rib and again he flinches, but this one isn't broken, either. He'd be making a much worse sound right now. "Were you at a museum or something when it hit?" I ask.

"No. I was at a dig site."

My hands stop. "A dig site? Like, archaeology?" I stand back, and he drops his hoodie back down.

The dinosaur guy rolls his eyes. "Yeah, like archaeology."

"I don't think any of your ribs are broken," I say. "You're just really bruised."

"Wow, thanks, doc. I'll be sure to take your word as gospel." Despite the tough talk, he's still using the tree for support.

I tilt my head. "What's your name?" If we're going to get out of here, I should at least know what to call him.

"Why do you care?" He squints at me. "So you can tell the cops where to find me?"

"Look. We're going to need to work together to get back out. So just tell me. I could already identify you to the cops if I needed to. You're pretty easy to pick out of a crowd."

He chews on that for a moment. Finally he says, "Lester. It's an old dude's name. A tribute to my mom's dad."

That's a surprising amount of information. I hold out my hand to shake. "I'm Remy. Named after the X-men character."

His eyebrows jump, pushing his ridges back. "You're named after Gambit?"

"Both my parents are big nerds. So are you, apparently."

His chuckle is hearty and deep. "I haven't always been robbing gas stations."

I'm starting to wonder about that now. Why was an archaeologist who likes comic books trying to throw down in my convenience store?

"What happened to you?" I ask.

His face closes up, like a shoelace pulled tight. "Nothing. Just hard times, you know?"

"No, I don't know." I was fine after the asteroid. Now he's half Allosaurus, and I can't imagine how that feels. "Not like you."

I thought he might get angry, but instead Lester's head droops. "I just couldn't handle it." He's no longer looking at me. "I broke down. Couldn't do my job. They took pity on me for a while, but once I got into drugs, it was easy to let me go."

Oh. So that's how he ended up here. "I think I can guess the rest."

Grunting with effort, Lester pulls himself up straight and stretches out his arms—but then he doubles over again. I wrap an arm around his side to help him stay upright.

"Thanks," he says, then shakes his head furiously. "Wait. I shouldn't be thanking you. You're the reason I'm here."

"Reminding you once again that you're the one who tried to rob my store." I point ahead of us, down the length of the ravine. "We can't get out by going straight up. We'll have to walk a ways until it gets shallower, by the river."

Lester huffs out a weary sigh. "You have to be kidding."

We start to walk, Lester leaning on me even though I'm more than a foot shorter than he is, not including his ridges.

"Did you get the piercings before or after?" I ask.

"Before. The tats, too."

"So an archaeologist with piercings and tats."

"We're people, too!"

I can't help but laugh. I like how deep and gravelly his voice is. I like how he smells, his arm slung over my shoulder. Whatever deodorant he's got on, it was a good choice.

"Maybe this is your wake-up call," I say. "Being chased by a girl until you fall into a ravine."

At this, Lester falls silent. He looks like he regrets a lot of things. "Yeah. Maybe so." He swallows hard. "It's just... I don't feel like a man anymore. I can't even get girls, not like I used to."

That strikes me as unfair. He's still pretty hot. Strangely, bizarrely hot for being part dinosaur.

"Maybe you're not looking in the right places," I suggest.

This earns me an arched eyebrow. "Where should I be looking?"

I don't know. Right at me, I guess.

"Unconventional places. There must be, I don't know, a website for people who are into that kind of thing."

"Which website, pray tell?"

I can feel that I'm flushing, so I look away quickly. "Whatever. I'm sure it's out there."

But Lester just hums. After a few moments of charged silence, he says, "Are you talking about people like you?"

It's so blunt that I cringe. The mud squishes under my sneakers, getting into my socks. "Maybe."

Silence falls again, and it's full of some unidentifiable

tension. Then Lester comes to a stop, and I have to stop with him.

"What is it?" I ask. "Does it hurt more?"

He doesn't answer. His yellow eyes latch onto mine, and there's a grin pulling at the sides of his long snout. "No." He tilts his head down so our faces are suddenly very close together. "I'm just curious now, about this girl who has a thing for monsters."

My eyebrows pull together. "Monsters?" I ask. "You're not a monster. You're an Affected."

"I'm part dinosaur, Remy." He barks a sad, desperate laugh. "That's what I call a monster."

I wish he could see what I see—a guy with a pretty kissable face. A guy who could probably do some wicked things with that long tongue.

"And so what?" I ask. "You're still worthy of love and affection, no matter what you look like. And I rather like how you look."

The clever smirk falls from his face. I take that moment to lean upward and press my lips the front of his snout.

Lester jerks back in surprise. After a beat, he gapes down at me.

"Oh," I say, stepping backward, putting distance between us.

"Did you just...?" His brain is sorting through what I've done, and I'm not sure if he's coming to a good conclusion or not.

"I'm sorry." I bring my hand to my mouth. "I didn't mean to—"

His arms swoop around me and before I can regain my footing, he's brought me upward so my face is right in front of his. Lester captures my lips with surprising force, and immediately they part for his larger, scaly ones. His mouth is softer than I expected, and deft as it maneuvers around my lower lip, suckling it before moving on to my top one. I gasp into him and he swallows it up, his arms weaving even tighter around me, pulling my waist against his.

Wow. Who knew a dinosaur-guy would be so good at kissing? I'm sinking into him, chest-to-chest, hip-to-hip. Every movement of his lips is like a soft breath over hot coals that's slowly nursing them into flames. The moment his tongue slips into my mouth, my lower body clenches. Oh, that tongue—it mesmerizes me as it winds around mine, longer and slimmer and much more pointed. He grazes my lip with one of his sharp teeth and a moan escapes me. Instantly, his hold tightens, and the tips of his claws scrape the fabric of my shirt. I wonder what those claws would do to my skin, and blood rushes downward into the pond between my legs.

That's when I hear the sirens.

"Oh, shit," I mumble, pulling away from Lester. He blinks a few times, then those ridged eyebrows lower in suspicion.

"You called the police?" He draws back abruptly, and his hands fall away.

"Yes, but that was before—"

"Fuck." He doesn't let me finish, dragging a clawed hand over his face. "I'm so fucked."

"No, no." I put a hand on his chest, trying to stop his recoiling from me. "Look, we'll just tell them that—"

"There's video footage, isn't there?" Lester shrugs me off. "Damn. I'm so going to go to jail."

I need to stop this train wreck. "I'll make sure you won't," I say, as earnestly as I can. "It was a miscommunication. That's all. There's no video footage."

His head tilts towards me, still angry, but perhaps less so. "None?"

"None."

With a groan Lester turns away from me and starts to jog on

ahead. I have to run to catch up because his legs are so much longer than mine.

"Where are you going?" I ask him.

His answer is gruff. "To clean up this mess you've made."

"You're the one who put a gun to my face," I say, grabbing his sleeve to stop him, but he just yanks it away.

"So you keep reminding me." But the words are laced with shame.

I grumble. "I feel like it's an important piece of context to keep in mind."

Lester just continues on ahead, the ravine widening out ahead of us. Police lights flash against the trees. I want to salvage this, because I've never felt anything like what I felt when his tongue invaded me. Now all I can imagine is how else he might fit inside me. But he's closed off completely as we reach the shallow end of the ravine and it seems there's no going back.

The cops take our statements. I admit to panicking a little when Lester came into the store with his head covered. He admits to carrying two boxes of Milk Duds in his pocket that looked like a gun. What they don't know is the real gun is still somewhere out in the woods, tucked under a tree.

The sheriff's pissed at me for placing a call when I supposedly didn't need to, and confused as to why we emerged from the woods together while two customers were waiting at the door to be served. Anyone could have stolen anything while I was gone. I'm sure word will get back to my boss, and then I'll lose the job anyway—but I'm not going to be the one to tell him what happened tonight.

No camera, no evidence.

Now that the cops are done with us, Lester leaves and I run to talk to him before he can get in his car.

"Wait. Please." The backs of my eyes burn when I think of him hating me as he leaves tonight. "I'm sorry." I don't know why I'm apologizing when, again, he's the one who held a gun to my face and demanded I open the register. But I don't want this to end here, right when it felt like a light had appeared at the end of the tunnel after all these years.

Lester doesn't look at me as he opens the car door. "It's fine," he says. "At least I'm not going to jail tonight. That's what matters." He slams it closed behind him and starts up the engine. The car sputters angrily.

"Come on." I lean in the open window so he can't pull away just yet. "You're acting like nothing happened."

"Nothing did happen, did it?" he asks, and those reptilian eyes focus on mine. They are hard and unyielding. "It was no big deal."

"No big deal?" It felt like a big deal—to me, at least.

"Right." He waves me off. "Now can I go, please? We've been dealing with the cops for an hour now and I want to crash."

So that's it. The light in the tunnel winks out as I withdraw from the window. Lester starts rolling it up.

"If you change your mind," I say, "you know where to find me."

The window pauses for a second. Then, with a resigned sigh, he closes it the rest of the way, and the car pulls out.

I didn't know him at all, but it still feels like someone sliced my heart in half.

Luckily, my boss doesn't find out about me calling the cops, or about the customers who might have gone in and swiped whatever they wanted while I was out gallivanting through the woods. Not that it makes working there any better.

At least now I have something I want, something that drives me in my off time. I do a little research online, and then build a forum called "Dating for the Affected," where I hope people like Lester can go to find some romance in their lives. I create a profile for myself, of course, and make the very first post on the website: "Looking for a reptile to show me a good time."

It takes a few weeks for anyone to find the site, but once they do, word starts to spread quickly. I get a few messages— one from a girl who merged with her pet iguana, another from a guy who was at a zoo when the asteroid hit and became half-komodo dragon. I go out with both of them, but there's no spark at all and the dates end without exchanging phone numbers.

Within two months, an influencer Affected who merged with a chimpanzee posts to TikTok about the message board, and suddenly it's swarmed. Affecteds from all over the world start to post, and it isn't long before they're finding matches. The site gets overloaded as word spreads and the domain host starts demanding I pay more money to host the surge of traffic —which of course, I can't afford. A few regular users make donations to help cover it, and for a while, the site continues on.

That's when someone makes the app. They use the same name as my forum, and almost immediately, my traffic drops off to nothing. No one needs the message board anymore. Reluctantly I close the website, and once again the tunnel stops at a dead-end. The one thing I tried to do to make myself forget about Lester, and still I can't get him out of my mind.

I hope he's okay, and that he's found a way around robbing convenience stores to crawl out of whatever hole he'd dug for himself. After resisting and resisting, I finally download the app to my phone and create an account. I'm not sure what I'm expecting to get out of it—maybe I'm just curious. Maybe I want to find my perfect match.

Maybe I'm hoping to come across Lester.

Every day I check for new possible matches, but still no sign of him. Then one afternoon, I'm late for my shift at the gas station, and that's it for me. I'm toast.

Time to find a new job, again.

The iguana girl I'd met through the forum matches with me on the app, and we agree to meet up a second time as friends. She's a waitress at a nearby Olive Garden that happens to be in desperate need of a host. With her recommendation I slide right through the hiring process. Maybe the wages are shit, but at least they're wages, and I'll survive until I make my next mistake.

One Friday evening—the worst night of the week to be hostessing—a familiar man with yellow eyes and greenish scales walks in. There's a human woman on his arm, clutching it close and talking quickly in his ear as they come inside. I can hear the app name slide off her tongue. That must be how they met.

Lester's eyes connect with mine immediately and his jaw slackens. I do my best to summon up my hostess smile in spite of the heavy stone in my belly.

"There's a little bit of a wait tonight," I say. "About twenty-five minutes."

The woman huffs. "Huh? What are we supposed to do for half an hour?"

"You're welcome to sit at the bar if there's room," I offer.

She just huffs again. "C'mon, Lester. Let's go somewhere else where they're willing to give us a table."

But Lester is quiet, still focused on me. Then he shakes his head like he's trying to remember where he is and what he's doing. "We should just wait," he tells her. "It's not that long."

I have to admit that he looks good. Great, even. He's wearing a black leather jacket to go with his spiked collar, and the shadowy grooves under his eyes are gone.

The woman tugs his arm. "Let's go. I didn't even want to come to Olive Garden."

"But the breadsticks..." Lester begins.

"I don't care about the breadsticks. I can't even eat bread."

He rolls his eyes. "You can, you just choose not to."

The woman throws her arms up in frustration, then turns and heads out the door. Lester doesn't follow. Instead he turns back to me, and his eyes traverse me from head to toe in a way that distinctly reminds me of our moment in the ravine together.

"Hey," I say, my voice trembling a little. How has he made me this nervous?

"Hey," he responds. "I, uh, didn't think I would see you again." He seems less angry than I expected after the last time, when he put his whole foot down on the gas pedal and sped out of the parking lot.

"Yeah. Same." Surreptitiously I pick up a menu. "Don't you want to go after your date? She's leaving."

He gives a disaffected shrug. "She was sort of a hassle."

I find myself fiddling with the menu. "Oh. Okay. Well, if you want to stay, I think there is one seat at the bar."

His tail swishes behind him, and I wish I knew what that meant. Lester's reptilian face doesn't really give anything away.

"All right." He tilts his head at me as I pass him the menu. "When do you get off, Remy?"

Just the sound of my name on his lips sends a shudder through me. He remembered. Immediately I'm back in the ravine, sharing that kiss, feeling the way it lit up every nerve ending under my skin.

"Oh, um..." I trail off, because I'm not sure if I should tell him. That might be inviting him in, when I'm not sure I want to. "They send me home around ten."

Lester's lips peel back in a smile, revealing his long teeth. That familiar pink tongue emerges and he licks one of his fangs. "I'll wait," he says. "Find me later."

And with that he takes the menu and walks off to the other side of the restaurant, making a spot for himself at the bar. My mouth opens and closes a few times, not sure what's just happened or what he intends by it. It's a little presumptuous of him, after the way he treated me, to think I want to see him after work. The last thing I want is to be his second choice after his lame date dropped him.

Yet the rest of my shift drags by, bogged down by anticipation. I catch a glimpse of Lester's back whenever I leave the hostessing station. It's big and wide as he sits hunched over the bar with a drink in his hand. He's even cut neat holes down the back of his jacket for each of his ridges.

Finally, the clock hits ten and we lock up the doors. One of the waitresses tries to shoo Lester out for the night, but I quickly interrupt to explain that he's there for me. She glances between us with one eyebrow raised, then shrugs and walks off. I think that new app has already starting changing people's view of the Affected as potential romantic matches.

Lester stands up. I forgot just how tall he is. His fingers dance across my lower back as he nods towards the door.

"Could I take you out for a drink?" he asks. "There's a good place that's open late down the block."

I survey him carefully. So he's just going to go on another date after his first one of the night fell through? That doesn't make me feel great.

The best I can do is answer honestly. "I don't know, man. You might have lost your chance." I've had the opportunity in the time that's lapsed to feel that he was a little unjust towards me.

Lester's face falters. He was excited about this. He had to

have been, I suppose, to sit around waiting for me for the last few hours.

"Oh." The word is bitten off. "Yeah. That would make sense." He clenches his hands into fists and looks down at them like it's easier than looking into my face. "Guess I fucked up that night."

He couldn't have guessed that it made me feel disposable? Then again, he was in the middle of robbing a convenience store for a little extra cash just so he could get out of debt. It's not like he was in the best frame of mind.

"Can I at least buy you a drink to apologize?" he asks hopefully. "I owe you one. Or two. I would have been screwed that night if you hadn't lied to the cops for me."

He's right—he would have. To see it in that light now infuriates me more.

"Fine. But two drinks, your tab, and then I'm going home." As I turn to leave, Lester quickly jogs ahead so he can open it for me in a sad attempt at chivalry.

We make our way to the bar down the block in silence. Lester digs his hands deep into his pockets. He glances at me a few times, but when he sees I'm not interested in talking, he looks back down at the ground.

"Damn," he says after we've gotten our drinks and sat down. "I didn't realize I made you that mad."

And hurt, I think. I'm more hurt than I am mad.

"That sounds so shitty," I say, taking a big sip of my drink. "Like it's my fault that I'm angry and not yours. You were the one who zoomed out of there like you were on fire after kissing me better than anyone's kissed me in my life."

He perks up, and a dumb smile races across his face. "I did?"

I set my jaw. "Don't sound so proud of yourself. That's just what made it really mean when you bounced."

"Right." He chases an ice cube with his straw. "I'm sorry. It wasn't great of me to take off like that and pretend nothing happened."

So now he's caught up.

"Yup," I say.

We fall quiet again. I finish up my drink, and Lester leaves to get us each another one. This clearly isn't going how he'd hoped.

After another pregnant silence he says, "I guess I thought you liked me."

"I did."

He chews on his lip and I wonder if he ever cuts himself with his teeth by accident. "Right."

"We barely know each other," I say. "Like you said back then, it's not that big of a deal." It was for me, though. I think about that kiss every single night. Sometimes I drop my hand down between my thighs remembering it, and pull my toys out of my bedside table remembering it.

Lester leans in a little, curiously searching my face. "I don't think that's true."

If he knows I've done nothing but think about him since then, that gives him leverage, and I don't need anyone else to have leverage over me.

"It certainly seems like it wasn't a big deal for you," I say. "I worked at that gas station for another five months. You could have come back any time."

"To the scene of my crime?" he asks. "No way."

"And then you got on that dating app, apparently."

A sharp gust of air bursts from his nostrils. "Yeah. I did. I was looking for you."

I want to believe this is true. "Then how come we never matched?" I ask. I had clearly put in my profile that I was into reptiles.

That's when I realize: He's no reptile. He's a *dinosaur.*

It's like Lester can read the look right off my face. He stifles a chuckle behind one clawed hand. "You didn't."

I've been barking up the wrong tree for weeks. I groan. "My preferences probably filtered you out!" God, I'm such an idiot, and this whole time I've been mad at *him*.

But he doesn't look upset—in fact, he's leaning forward on the table toward me, eyes twinkling. "Can we start over? Could we pretend this is date number one?"

"I guess we could," I say. Lester doesn't seem like he's going to let me get away without a fight, but if he wants me, he's going to have to get on his knees and beg.

"Great," he says, relieved. "That would be great."

It's actually a fun date. Lester introduces himself to me as if for the first time, and it's so charming that I giggle like a kid. I wish I was wearing anything besides a dress shirt and slacks.

"I promise I don't dress so square all the time," I say. "Just at work."

"Now I'm curious what you wear the rest of the time." He leans his long head on one hand. "Hopefully you'll let me take you out again to see it."

Of course that's what I want, but I shouldn't seem too eager. "All right. I'll allow it."

He grins. "Good."

We talk about our childhoods, our likes and dislikes, and the endless breadsticks at Olive Garden. He tells me a little about his former job but skips over the part in the middle where he was robbing convenience stores for emergency cash. Now he's working at Home Depot, moving lumber and helping customers find what they're looking for. I'm not surprised. He has the build for it. "It's that time of year when everybody is building garden boxes out front," he says.

I remember a time when I'd dreamed about owning my own place, having a yard, and growing some food in it. That feels impossible now.

"Are you okay?" he asks, leaning towards me. "Do you need another drink?"

I'm already feeling a little tipsy, so I shake my head. "No. Just thinking how I keep ending up in these dead-end jobs. It's not really how I imagined my life."

Lester nods in understanding. "This isn't really how I pictured my life turning out, either."

"You had a good job before. Can't you get back into archaeology now that you're sober?"

He just sighs wistfully and finishes off his drink. "They won't take me back. I'm stuck here now. At best maybe I could get a job as a museum tour guide."

I try to return some levity to the conversation. "You would have the inside scoop on dinosaurs."

This earns me a little smile. "That's true."

He pays the tab, then returns and offers me an elbow. I happily take it, and when we leave the bar, I'm relieved to breathe in some fresh air.

Lester steps to one side and pulls me along with him, and then before I know it, I'm in his arms again. He's looking down at me over the long ridge of his snout, nostrils flaring. "One thing about being me," he says, "is I can smell so much better now. And I'm glad for that because you smell great."

I blink. "Really? But I've been sweating at work all day."

"Exactly." He lowers his head so our mouths are only a few inches apart. "I like it. They say that's how you know when you're compatible with someone—you like the smell of their sweat."

I have to laugh. He's charming when he wants to be. "I've never had anyone say they like how my sweat smells."

"First time for everything."

47

I find myself staring at his lips again, wondering how they would feel this time.

"I'd really like to kiss you," he says, and then his voice drops lower. "Again."

We might have been pretending this was a first date, but maybe not anymore now that we're wrapped up together against the wall of the bar.

"Okay," I say, tamping down the excitement in my voice. "I'd like that."

It's just as good this time, if not better. His mouth is firmer, hungrier, and his long tongue plays lovely games with mine inside my mouth. He even gently runs the tip of his teeth over my lip, and a little groan escapes him.

"God, you are a great kisser," he says once we finally pull apart. He licks his chops. "I could do this all night."

I find that I'm not opposed to that idea. "I could, too." The bar door opens and a few drunk girls stumble out together, giggling as their Uber pulls up. "But maybe we should go somewhere a little more private?"

A flash of mischief crosses Lester's face. "What do you have in mind?"

I'm not sure what his place is like, but mine is a dingy little basement room in a big shared house. Taking him back there feels pathetic. "Your place, maybe?"

"I'm down with that, but we'll have to be quiet. My roommate works early."

Immediately I start thinking about what sort of things we could do that would require me to be quiet, and my stomach somersaults. The warm place between my thighs tightens just imagining it.

"Okay. I... I can be quiet."

His lips lift on one side, and he nods down the street. "I'm that way. We can walk there, if you want. It's about a quarter mile."

The words of agreement get stuck in my throat, so instead I just nod. Lester takes my hand in his as we start down the sidewalk, his claws curling around my knuckles, and something about it feels safe and warm.

His apartment is up on the second floor of a big brick building. It's nothing fancy, and the railings on the stairs are falling apart. Maybe I didn't need to feel so ashamed of my place when we're both just making a life where we can. There's something comforting about his struggle to open the door, twisting the knob one way and the other before it finally opens.

"Can't get the landlord to fix anything," he grumbles.

He leads me inside and almost immediately we're on the couch, lips locked together. He gently pushes me down, and brackets my head between his arms so he doesn't crush me. Now I can feel his hips against mine, and there's a definitive lump in his jeans that's pressing insistently against my thigh.

So I turn him on, do I? The idea fills me up with a warm longing, a need for more than just fervent kisses. Boldly I rub my pelvis against his, and Lester groans into my mouth.

"Oh?" He returns the gesture, and that tantalizing shape inside his pants rubs up and down between my legs. "You like that, do you?"

"Do you?" I shoot back. He chuckles and leaves my mouth to kiss my throat.

"I've been thinking about you ever since that night." His sultry tone makes me think that perhaps he's been imagining me the same way I've been imagining him. He grazes his fangs over my skin and I gasp in response.

"Yeah," I whisper. "I've been thinking about it, too."

It's been ages since I've been intimate with anyone. I haven't felt the rush, the need, or the desire like I do now. I want to know what's underneath Lester's leather jacket and tight jeans. Is he scaly all over? And what does *it* look like?

"Can we...?" I clear my throat awkwardly. "Does everything, um, work?"

He blinks in confusion a few times before it dawns on him what I'm asking. This time when he smiles, he bares his sharp teeth.

"Do you want to find out?"

I have to stop myself from nodding furiously, because all I want is to keep feeling him on top of me but without clothing between us. Instead I say, "Yeah. I do."

With surprising haste, Lester hops up from the couch and offers his hand. I let him lead me down the hall to his room, which is small but covered to the gills in décor. There are band posters for punk bands everywhere, spreads of superheroes in action, and even a pair of what look like antique daggers hung up over his desk. His closet is open and all of his clothes are some variation of black.

"Sorry it's a little messy," he says, quickly wiping dirty laundry off the bed, but I feel comfortable here. It reminds me of my own room with the bed perpetually unmade and doing double-duty as a hamper.

"Please, don't worry." I sit down on the edge, running my hand over the quilt. It's nice, and looks homemade. "My room isn't much better."

Lester is a little stiff as he settles down next to me on the bed. He's nervous, which I find sweet. This time I make the first move, turning towards him so I can run a hand down his chest. I stop at his abdomen, where a heavy black belt with studs stands between me and his steadily growing hard-on. I glance up at him, looking for permission, and he gives me a nod of encouragement. His nostrils are flared, yellow eyes fixated on my face.

The first thing I note when I tease my fingers over his groin is just how big he is under there, and again my lower half clenches in anticipation. Suddenly I want to hurry through all this foreplay stuff. What if he just pushed me down on the bed and shoved himself inside me?

But no, this is our first time. I should take it slow.

As I caress the length under his pants, Lester's breathing speeds up. His cool hands find their way under my shirt, and the crispness of his claws brushing over my skin makes me gasp. Already I'm longing to get us both naked, to skip over all this boring undressing stuff. I've undressed him in my mind enough times.

"Lester." His eyes drop down to my mouth as I say his name, and again he licks his lips. "Will you take my clothes off?"

"Oh, god." The exclamation is breathed out as one word. "Yes, please."

His slow exploration of my belly becomes a hurried swoop to pull off my shirt. I know I have decent-sized boobs, but the look that comes over him when he sees them is better than I could've expected. His grin goes up high on both sides of his snout, and his nostrils flare even wider. He reaches around behind me to take off my bra, then a frown takes over as he struggles with the catch.

"Damn it," he growls. "Stupid claws."

"I like them." I take over for him, pulling the band apart so it falls loose over my chest. With one finger he slides the strap down my arm, and he shows even more of his teeth as I'm exposed to him. My nipples are already so hard that they ache.

Leaning forward, he cradles each of my breasts in his hand, one after the other. While he touches me, scraping his claws over my nipples, he drags his lips down my throat to my collar. I whimper underneath him, and he chuckles.

"I've barely touched you and you're already reeking of sex," he says. "It's so hot, Remy."

It's beyond embarrassing that he can smell that, but it doesn't seem to bother him, so I melt into his touch. He lifts my breast and takes my nipple between his lips, gently running that tantalizing tongue over it until I'm gasping.

"Lester," I manage out. "Will you take yours off, too?"

He makes one last pass with his mouth and then leans back, shrugging off his jacket first, then peeling up his shirt. Scales cover his toned body, and he has no nipples to speak of—which makes sense, I suppose.

This time when he slides his arm around my back, it's to lie me back on his bed. He hovers over me, his huge tail thrashing back and forth.

"God, you're so hot." He runs his hands down my belly, his claws igniting beads of pleasure along the way. He undoes the button of my slacks and grabs onto the hem, and I lift my butt so he can pull them off. He takes the band of my underwear with them so suddenly I'm exposed. His hands continue down my hips, over my thighs, all the way to my knees. A slick of drool has pooled under his fangs. "I can't wait to lick you up."

At this idea my whole body shivers, and that slow heat bursts into a frantic flame. It's his hand that ventures there first, and the moment his cool claw brushes over my clit, I let out a moan. Chuckling, he leans down to kiss me, hard.

"Remember," he whispers against me, "quiet."

"Right." I try to keep this at the forefront of my mind as he makes a second pass over my clit, earning another muffled moan, then drags his finger downward to the wet slit waiting for him there. He curls his finger and nuzzles it with his knuckle, and he lets out a groan of his own.

"You're so wet, my god." Lester's breathing quickens as he tests me, bringing that wetness up through my swollen folds.

Then he ducks his head down and before I can speak, he has his huge mouth between my legs. I cover my face to hold in another moan as finally that wonderful, delicious tongue comes out. Soon I'm writhing underneath him as it torments my clit and then sweeps down to lick up all the juices that have gathered beneath it.

My hips buck as that tongue slips inside me, and even from behind my hand I can't stop the noise that comes out. He fucks me with his mouth hard, then returns to my clit, again and again. I've never felt anything like it. Bright lights shoot off in my vision as he licks and sucks and flicks.

"Fuck," I whisper. "I'm going to come."

"Good." His pace speeds up and soon I'm clenching one of his ridges in my hands, trying to swallow my cries as I careen into oblivion. No vibrator could imitate that.

When he's finished between my legs and I'm lying there like a limp toy, he unbuckles his belt and tosses it to the side. The button of his jeans comes next, and then the zipper. Oh, I finally get to see it—and, if all continues to go well, feel it.

Underneath he's wearing black boxers covered in skulls, and now his huge cock can finally breathe. It tents the boxers, trying to slide through the slit at the front. I'm too impatient. I duck my fingers into the hem of the boxers and pull them down, allowing the tent pole underneath to spring free.

"Oh my god." I can't help the exclamation. Lester suddenly recoils from me, squeezing his legs together.

"What?" he asks, defensive. "What is it?"

Not only is he huge, but it looks like nothing I've ever seen before, emerging from a long opening at his groin. The same ridges that run along his eyebrows and neck also decorate his cock, and it has soft, perfectly smooth scales covering it all the way to the head. Underneath I can see skin, and a bead of pre-come coats the slit at the very tip.

"It's awesome," I say, not really thinking twice about my words before they come out. I sit up so I can reach towards him, and though he tenses up, Lester doesn't move away. I'm gentle with my fingers, testing the heft of him, and he stifles a grunt as I wrap my whole hand around it.

Briefly, I wonder if he'll actually fit inside of me, and this sends a cascade of anticipation directly into my pussy. I can't wait to find out.

"You... like it?" Lester asks, voice full of shame and uncertainty.

"Oh, I do." I squeeze gently as I drag my hands up and then down again. He clenches the sheets in his claws. "Very much."

His relief comes out as a long exhale. "I know it's weird and everything—"

"So?" I pump my hands again and he shudders. "It's you." I pull the scaly skin down this time, admiring the pinkish head that slides out from underneath it. I drop down to my hands and knees, and Lester gasps with surprise before I even touch his crown with my tongue.

"Fuck," he hisses, a hand tangling in my hair as I gently take it into my mouth. "That's incredible."

I've barely gotten started. Realizing that I'm probably the first person he's been with since he became an Affected, I decide to pay close attention to his pleasure, to make him feel desired and accepted. I swallow him up and his hips buck into my mouth, nearly gagging me. My lips can barely stretch wide enough to fit. I continue to pump him in time with my hands and soon he's fallen back on his elbows, muscled belly flexing and arching with each of my thrusts.

"Remy," he grunts. "If you keep doing that, I'm going to come in your mouth."

I pause my assault on his beautiful cock. "Do you want that?"

After a few deep breaths he says, "I'd much rather do it inside you."

Oh. A boiling wave of desire rolls through me at the thought. "Can... can you, like, get me...?" It's too awkward to say the whole thing out loud.

Lester gets a rueful look on his face. "No. We're sterile. Just another side-effect." But it transforms into a wicked grin, and he sits up so he's towering over me. "Which means I can fill you up all I want."

Suddenly I'm flat on my back and he's pinning my wrists down to the bed. Lester's reptilian pupils are dilated and heavy with need as he licks his teeth. I have to have more, so I arch my back to run my pelvis over his beautifully swollen cock, showing him what I want. He *tsks*.

"So eager and naughty." Releasing one of my wrists, he reaches down to press his length down between my legs. There's a burst of sensation right where the soft head of him makes contact with my clit, and I bite my lip to keep from making a sound. "That's right," he whispers, his fangs settling by my ear. "Stay quiet while I make you mine."

It's so predatory, so primal that my lower half draws in tight, imagining his phantom cock filling me up. I wonder how much the melding has changed how his brain works, if fucking me is an animalistic urge as much as a human one.

"Yes," I whisper back. "I'll be quiet."

I'm so slick when he brings himself down between my soft, swollen lips that he slides easily between them, just dragging those scales over my clit until I'm practically begging him with the snap of my hips to dive down further. His other claw doesn't release my wrist as he finally nudges at me, willing my small slit to open for him. When I gasp, it does, and he seizes this opening to press inside.

"Oh!" I can't hold it in as he's finally there, right where I want him, finally making me open up. With surprising self-control Lester pauses, then starts to drag his cock around in a gentle circle, encouraging my tight, wet channel to relax for him. I can tell all he wants is to fuck me now, fast and hard, but he's not going to rush into it. I admire his discipline.

But I want more. I need more. Every muscle is flexing, trying to draw him in, hoping to complete this mission we've started. Somewhere deep down is an empty pool that needs filling, and only he can deliver it.

"More," I say. "More, please." With each movement the ridges on his cock stimulate something new, something even more sensitive than before. Lester curls his arms around my head, brings his fangs down to my throat, and obliges.

The explosion of sound and color when he thrusts all the way in overwhelms me. I press my mouth to his shoulder to hold in my moans. He's there, right where I need him, and it's far beyond anything I could have dreamed up in my fantasies.

"Damn," Lester says, sitting back so he can admire our bodies where they're joining together, his cock spreading my lower lips wide. "You feel so fucking good, I can't believe it." He remains like that, gripping my thighs in his claws, as he begins to stroke.

"Oh, god." I fall back down to the bed, lost to the feel of him, the breadth of him, the fulfillment of him. His claws rove over my belly, my breasts, my nipples as he continues his slow conquest, remaining deep and thick and delicious. It's only once I'm dripping wet and my back is arched to the sky that he starts to draw himself out, so only the tip anchors us together, and then plunges back in. I bite down hard on my lip to keep a cry from coming out, and Lester lets out a deep, rumbling chuckle.

"Good girl," he says, petting my hair with one hand while the other keeps my arm pinned. But now that he's given me some I want more and more. Those sweet, perfect ridges and the soft, textured scales—I'm already so close to the edge that I wonder if I'll live through this.

"Lester," I whimper, lifting my hips so I can take him even further in, welcoming him inside me.

"Do you want more, beautiful?" he asks, lifting me up by my rump. The angle changes and I can't help the cry that bursts out of me as he thrusts again, hard. The cheap bed frame squeaks with each stroke, bumping the wall with each tremor that travels through our connected bodies. He offers me his hand and I bite down on it as he begins pumping with a powerful vigor. I've never been so turned on in my life, like his cock is on a waterslide, those luscious ridges thrumming inside my body as he shoves himself into the depths. I'm lost to the avalanche of sensation striking at my neck and spreading throughout my body with the beat of my blood.

"Oh, fuck," I moan into his hand. My climax hovers just on the edge of my vision, dancing closer as Lester plunders me with his gorgeous, strange, wonderful cock. He leans down close, and the edges of his sharp teeth drag down my throat as his tongue caresses my skin.

"I'm going to fill you up," he growls, panting against my ear. "Are you ready, Remy?"

I'm so close that I worry I might just combust. I frantically nod, and Lester grunts with satisfaction. His arms wind tight around my body to pull me flush against his, and this is perhaps the closest I've ever felt to another person. His claws clench my ass and his fangs graze my ear. The room is awash with the scent of our sweat, our sex, our heavy breathing.

I'm rising, drifting higher and higher until I'm so tight that each thrust squelches, his cock dragging against my clenching inner walls. I bury my face in Lester's neck, holding onto him with every ounce of my strength because otherwise, the agonizing pleasure he's doling out to me like Christmas presents might simply sweep me away into space.

"Yes," he murmurs into my ear, raspy and animalistic. "Yes, sweetheart."

When it hits me every last muscle in my body goes wire-tight, as if it's desperately trying to hold itself together. Lester groans against my throat, whispering my name over and over. I'm cascading and soon he's coming along with me, pounding me with a force like nothing I've felt before. Then he bursts, his hot flood filling me up so full it starts to drip out around him.

Lester collapses on top of me, barely holding himself up with one elbow. His bright yellow eyes are half-closed as he nuzzles my forehead with his snout, pressing one kiss after another to my brow, my cheek, my nose, my mouth. The way he slips one arm under my head and brings me close to his neck, I wonder if something new and tender has begun between us.

Somebody bangs on the wall, followed by a loud grumble of annoyance.

"So much for being quiet," Lester says with a chuckle. The ring in his nostril tickles my face. "But I liked hearing you moan."

"I liked everything," I say.

He takes a deep whiff of me, then sighs. "I never thought I'd come across someone like you."

I have to admit I feel the same way, for very different reasons. He felt that being Affected made him unlovable, while I believed being a loser did the same for me. But maybe neither of us are what we think we are. Maybe we just needed to find each other.

Eventually he has to withdraw, and I'm shocked by the gush of come that leaks out of me. But Lester grabs a box of tissues from his bedside table and mops me up, then pulls me into his hot-blooded embrace. He yawns against my hair, and a little of it gets caught in his teeth.

"Oops." He plucks it out. "Guess I'm going to have to figure out being around a girl like this."

I sigh and sink into him. "You don't need to do anything. You're perfect."

As we fall asleep like that, I feel as if life has taken a sudden left turn. My trajectory has changed, and I may never be the same.

Lost in the Snow

I GUESS YOU COULD SAY I'M A "RECRUITER."

My technical job title is "Field Responder." That is, I answer calls out in the field when someone with my skill set could be useful. I'm somewhere between a hostage negotiator and a saleswoman. I talk down monsters that might otherwise not be open to what I have to offer. But I'm good at talking. I've been doing this a long time.

The flight to Alaska is lengthy but not boring because I always bring two books when I travel, one for each direction. Before I know it I'm descending into Anchorage, marveling at how everything is white with snow even though it's April.

I pick up my rented car and summon the instructions I wrote down on my phone. GPS could lead me astray on these backroads, and it might not even know some of them exist. I'm headed to a ranch, whose name I've already forgotten, where my potential client is waiting. It'll take a few hours to get out there.

Snow drifts down in gentle, tiny flakes, so I put on my music and drive. I follow the directions, trying to remember how many roads I've passed since most of them don't even have signs.

There. I take a right and the car jumps as I hit a pot hole. It's another few miles down this road until farm equipment starts to come into view. A few trucks are parked outside the house, and my little sedan pulls in neatly between two of them.

When I go up to the house and knock, though, no one answers.

I hear shouting in the distance. That must be where they are with the potential client. I head off towards the sound, wishing I'd worn something a little more sturdy. These booties are not cutting it in snow that's two feet deep.

"Get back!" There's a loud *clang* as someone hits a metallic object. There's a roar of answer, and I already know this particular negotiation is going to start off on the wrong foot.

Around the side of the barn, three men stand with long guns in their hands. One is banging a metal cage with the butt of his weapon, shouting, "Get back!"

Something inside the cage moves. It's big, bigger than either of the men, and when it roars and lunges at the bars of the cage, its thick hair moves with it.

Hair. I'm probably dealing with a yeti.

"Back up, guys," I call out. In their surprise, one of the men points his gun at me, and I raise my hands up. "Hey, watch where you point that thing. You're the one who called me." I pause. "Well, you called the cops. And then they called me because they don't want to get anywhere near a monster. Is that right?"

The men grunt in agreement.

"You?" one of them says when I approach. "Just a little lady? How are you gonna help us?"

I may be small, but I'm good at my job. Sometimes it even helps me a little. Everyone underestimates me.

"I'm Rena Summers, from the Monster Menagerie."

One of the men snaps his fingers and says, "Oh, I know them."

"Right. So what happened here?" I step toward the cage. "Why don't you guys just back away and everybody can take a deep breath, all right?"

"That thing's been eating our cows," one of the men growls, lowering his rifle. "I finally caught it, though. Walked right into my trap."

I ignore him and take in the yeti's condition. He's dirty, I'll give him that. But this bear cage wasn't really clean to start with.

"Hey," I say to the yeti, stepping towards the bars. He has bright golden eyes, and his face is still visible under the shower of white hair. He has a firm mouth pulled down at the sides, and a flat nose better suited to cold conditions. He towers over me, even more than most people do. "What's your name?" I ask him.

One of the men laughs. "That thing can't talk or it would have by now."

I roll my eyes. Everyone assumes monsters who live off the grid somehow don't have the ability to speak. But with the exception of the less humanoid creatures, most monsters can talk in some shape or form. There's a sharkman at the Menagerie who uses sign language in his tank.

The yeti grunts and shakes his head.

"See?" the second man says. "Not a word."

"Ignore them," I tell the creature. "Do you want to get out of here?" I say it like we've just met at a bar and I want to go home together. "We can just ditch this place. I know somewhere way better."

The yeti just grumbles and moves to the back of the cage. I need to make him understand somehow that what I'm offering is better than this.

I don't just work for the Menagerie because it's a job. I like monsters. I respect them. I want them to have the best possible life they can in this world we've taken from them. I wouldn't do this if I didn't believe it was right.

"What about my cows?" the first man asks, gesturing with his gun. "He'll just come back. He's already killed three of 'em."

I can't negotiate with my potential client while these numbskulls are here.

"If I can successfully convince our friend to come with me, the Menagerie will help cover the cost of your lost livestock." This isn't true, but I need them to leave me alone with him. "But I can't do that with you here. He's afraid of you."

"As well he should be!" One of the other men sounds a little drunk. "If I ever see him here again, I'm gonna—"

"We get the picture," I tell him. "Now go on. I'll take care of this. Okay?"

The men complain, but eventually one of them surrenders the key to me and they all stalk back to the house. One shoots a warning shot into the air, and both the yeti and I cover our ears.

Finally they're gone. "Sorry about them," I say, approaching the bars. "It's just you and me now. Can we talk a little?"

"No reason," the yeti says quietly. I almost can't hear him, so I lean even closer. "Let me go."

"The only way those men are going to let you go is if you're going with me," I say. "I assume you were swiping livestock because you're hungry. Is that right?"

The yeti says nothing, but his lips turn down in a scowl.

"Right. There's not much to eat in winter, is there? But if you chose to go with me back to the Menagerie, you'd never be hungry again. Three square meals a day, if you want. Or two. Whatever your body prefers."

The yeti might look like he isn't listening, but I can see when he cocks his head ever-so-slightly.

"Do you want me to open the cage door?" I ask. "So we can talk properly?"

There's a long pause, and then, he nods his head.

"Great." I put the key in the lock and turn, so it pops open. "Now don't run off, okay? I want us to have a conversation."

Slowly, the yeti starts to move in my direction. I keep my hands where he can see them, staying in front of the door opening so he can't simply bolt past me. I need to earn his trust first, and show him I'm not trying to do anything that's against his will. He'll have to come freely.

The Monster Menagerie is a voluntary program, providing monsters with residential homes in exchange for a little show-and-tell. They're asked to spend a few hours a day in their exhibition rooms behind bulletproof plastic walls, so people touring the Menagerie can observe them in their "natural habitats." It's the perfect safe haven for a creature like this yeti, who isn't doing well out in the wild anymore and has found himself running aground of humans. Humans are monsters' greatest threat, and our goal at the Menagerie is to offer them a respite, a safe haven.

"I'm here as a friend," I say as the yeti hovers at the open door. "I want to help you. I think you deserve a better life than scrounging the few offcuts you can get from these guys."

The yeti's gold eyes are watching me intently. I think he's listening.

"We'll give you a nice apartment that resembles your ideal lifestyle," I continue. "You can set the temperature as cold as you want and there's lots of entertainment and recreation." I try not to sound like a brochure and keep it personable.

The yeti makes a *hmph* sound, like he's hearing what I'm saying but doesn't believe me.

"It won't be the same," I add. "But it'll sure beat getting left in a cage or shot by one of these jokers." I gesture with my thumb at the house behind me.

I think that perhaps I'm getting through, until suddenly the yeti moves. And boy does he *move*. He's like a bolt of lightning as he shoves past me, out the door of the cage. But my stupid booties are stuck in the snow, so I stumble and fall, hitting my head on the metal bars.

For a second, the yeti stops and turns back to look at me.

"Fuck," is all I can say as I rub my head. Then I look up at him. "Please, don't go. Those guys will find you, and they'll kill you." I guess I don't have a filter anymore after getting such a sturdy bonk to the noggin.

Those golden eyes evaluate me for just a second longer, and then he's off running again through the snow.

Damn it. I was so close. Or was I? There's a good chance he just manipulating me and never intended to listen to my offer at all.

Great. I can't be the one responsible for letting him go, not when these assholes are ready to shoot off a gun at the sound of a snowflake falling. I only have one choice.

I tear off into the snow after him, booties be damned, and follow his huge footprints.

Being native to this region, obviously the yeti is much faster than I am. He has long vanished into the trees, but here I am still following in hope that he'll lead me to his home and we can have a longer conversation that isn't under duress. Maybe then he'll be more open to my proposition.

But as I finally reach the tree line, I feel the gentle flakes that have been falling turn thicker and heavier, each one landing on me like a fat raindrop. Great. Just great. I'm in Alaska, out in the middle of the wilderness while a snowstorm sets in.

I wonder what different life choices I could have made.

Still I keep on, because I have more determination to find the yeti than I do courage to face the men with guns. And I wasn't joking when I said they would probably kill him—it's my responsibility to help.

The snowfall steadily builds up on my shoulders as I keep walking, and so much snow has gotten in my booties and turned to water that my feet are squishing inside them with every step. God. I really wish I'd worn something else, something a tiny bit more practical. Now my toes are starting to freeze being submerged in cold water. As if the biting cold of the snow itself wasn't enough.

Luckily, it's easy to follow in the yeti's tracks, so I know I won't lose him. At least, I think I won't. The snow is starting to fall faster now, and it's filling up the gaps left by his huge, bare feet.

Oh, shit. I can't get lost out in the wild. I've gone at least a mile now, maybe two—there's no way those guys would find me.

That's when the tracks suddenly stop. I'm at the edge of a small pool, filled by a waterfall that's half-frozen over. There's white hair floating on the surface, as if the yeti was just here and then left before I could reach him.

Did he take a bath? In the middle of a snowstorm? I can only imagine what thick skin he has, how dense his hair must be to keep him warm out here.

Unfortunately, I have neither. I consider turning around to head back, but when I do...

My tracks are gone.

"Fuck," I say aloud. "Fuck fuck fuck." Now I've really made a mistake. If I can't find my way back, then the yeti is my only option. Maybe if I can find him, he'll be willing to get me back home, even if he decides not to go with me to the Menagerie. He seemed unfriendly, but not so cold as to let me die.

I hop over the little river that funnels off from the pool, and walk around the edge searching for prints. Finally, I find them, recent enough that they haven't been covered by the snow yet. I hurriedly take off after them, my feet squishing inside my socks and boots. I just hope that his bath has slowed him down and he's not much farther ahead.

But as the snowfall gets stronger and the cold bears down on me, I find I'm slowing. My teeth are chattering so hard I can feel the pounding up in my temple, and I'm curling and uncurling my hands to keep my fingers from freezing into claws. The tracks are starting to grow shallower and shallower, and soon they disappear.

I come to a stop. This can't really be how it ends for me, can it? It's idiotic, really. I was a high-powered career woman. I had a life trajectory planned out; get married in the next three years, maybe have a kid before I'm considered "geriatric," work my way up to a managerial position at the Menagerie, maybe even make it onto the board. I want to have the power to make decisions that will improve the lives of the monsters that live there.

"Hello?!" I call out, as loud as I can. If I cause an avalanche, so what? If I can't find help, my choice is to die out here alone or die under an avalanche. "Yeti? Are you there?!"

My voice carries a little, but the snowfall is killing my echo. I try again, even louder. "Hello! Somebody help me!"

No answer.

I try to keep walking in the direction of the prints I saw earlier, hoping that he kept in a straight line and didn't weave. But I'm getting sluggish now, my arms and legs shaking just as hard as my teeth, and I think my toes have gone completely to sleep. Maybe that means they're frostbitten, and I'm going to lose them in the long run.

Not that it matters if I don't survive this at all.

I don't notice when I trip on a rock, because my feet can't feel anything. It's when I topple forward, face-down in the snow, that I realize something has happened. Flailing, I manage to sit up, but now my feet won't work.

"Help!" I cry out again, but my voice is so weak. It would really just be a lot easier to go to sleep. Maybe, if I slept, I could feel warm again.

Is this what freezing to death is like?

I don't have any more *help*s left in me, so I sit there in the snow, trying to breathe. That's the last thing I remember.

"Fuck!" I awaken to a feverish, blistering pain in my feet. "Jesus!" Except my shouts don't come out as shouts but as ugly, hoarse groans.

"No move," a very stern voice warns me.

I blink a few times, but my eyes feel sticky and crusted. Moving my arms is a no-go. I can still feel most of them, but my hands and fingers? It's almost like they don't exist anymore.

I cry out again as searing pain rips through my foot and up my leg. Finally I crack my eyes open and look down to see what's happening to me.

My shoes have been taken off and lie a few feet away next to my soaking-wet socks. I'm sitting in front of a fire with my feet closest to the flame. There's a huge creature crouched over me, studying me intently.

It's the yeti. Wherever we are, I can't see much beyond the reach of the firelight, but I think it's a cave of some sort. There are scorch marks on the walls, along with some crude drawings. He must have come for me, out in the snow, and brought me back to his home.

Again my feet howl in agony, and I try to pull them away. The yeti roars.

"No move!" His voice is harsh, and immediately I stop what I'm doing. With an irritated sigh, he gestures at my feet. "Get warm. Or lose."

I suck in a breath. So I was that close to getting frostbite, or I still am. I check my arms and hands, where my fingers have turned a dark blue. That is definitely not a color skin should have.

"My hands!" I cry out, trying to move them. They don't respond more than a little twitch.

"Quiet," the yeti growls. He inches away from the fire, and reaches out with one big, furry arm to grab my hand. I'm too weak to fight back as he yanks it towards him, and presses my fingers between his huge palms.

Oh. There's that terrible pain again. I cry out and try to yank back, but the yeti is much stronger than I am, especially now.

"No move!"

I'm getting tired of hearing this, as much as he's probably getting tired of saying it. It's not like I have a choice, anyway, so I stop flailing, even though it feels like my whole body is on fire. I whimper and let my head fall back to the floor.

It's not hard, I realize. In fact, it's soft, as soft as a cloud. I turn my neck to one side and find fur brushing my face. It doesn't smell the best, but oh, does it feel good against my cold skin.

The yeti is watching me carefully, still holding my offending hand. Soon he lowers it back to the fur, and then gets to his feet. With heavy, lumbering footsteps he walks around me, then sits down on my right side and takes my other hand. It burns, too, but now I'm expecting the pain. I twitch and groan but try not to move, because the last thing I want is to get chastised by a yeti again.

While he sits there warming me up, I have no choice really but to stare at him. He's no longer dirty, not at all. In fact, his white fur is shining and somehow totally dry. It's not terribly long, about as long as the hair on a Persian cat, but it's thick and obscures most of the shape of his body. He doesn't say anything, so I keep staring, taking in as much as I can.

I love to learn about monsters, what their habitats are like, their natural diets, what makes them tick. They're all parts of the great tapestry that is our world, and frankly, the most interesting ones. I wonder if the yeti's hair works like polar bear hair. Does he have an undercoat? Does he shed in the summers? I have all sorts of questions, but I don't want to annoy him again.

Finally I ask, "What's your name?"

The yeti jerks a little, clearly surprised that I've broken the silence. Then his eyebrows lower.

"Why?"

"Well, I just thought that since you're helping me, I should know what to call you."

He looks even more agitated, but eventually he answers, "Morak."

"Morak," I repeat, to make sure I got the pronunciation right. With a grunt, he nods. "Wonderful. Morak. It's nice to meet you. I'm Rena."

He does not look interested at all in this information, but I don't mind. I'm used to talking when nobody around me cares to listen. "If I survive this," I say, and the yeti snorts, "then I really hope you'll consider my offer. Hell, even if I don't, my business card is in my pocket, and you should definitely call the Menagerie." Once again, he huffs with derision. I give him a stern look, trying to ignore the raging pain in my every limb. "I'm serious. I know you like your home, but lots of other, um, creatures live there, and they're all quite happy. I would be ecstatic to give you some testimonials." I cringe. "They're in my pocket."

Morak just rolls his eyes.

"What?" I ask. "What do you hate about the idea? Tell me. I want to know." I've been accused many times of being demanding, but it's just who I am. A dog with a bone, you might say.

He doesn't answer for a long time, and soon I begin to think he won't. But finally he lets out an irritated grunt and says, "Looking."

I'm thrilled that he's going to talk to me. I still have a shot at this. "Looking for what?"

He turns his face down towards me, and this time his eyes are sad. "Mate. Family."

Oh. Well, that's something we can't help with at the Menagerie, at least not until we get a call like this for another yeti. Even then, it's not like they'll just automatically be attracted to each other. They're not zoo animals.

"I see." I can't really offer him a solution to that particular problem. "Have you seen many of your kind recently?" I ask.

He looks away from me. "No."

Yetis must be endangered, like most of the monsters at the Menagerie. I know they tend to be isolated, so it's not as if anyone is keeping tabs on them or their population. This might be the first documentation we have.

My hand is still wedged between Morak's palms, and he's started absentmindedly stroking it. At least I have the feeling back in it now, even if it hurts.

"I'm sorry." I don't have a solution to offer, so I won't even try. "If it helps at all, there are billions of people on this planet and I still haven't found my mate, either."

He glances up at me with obvious surprise. "Why?" he asks, and I think there's a tinge of envy in his voice. "So many."

I nod. "Yeah. I mean, I've gone out with plenty of guys. But all of them are turned off by me. If I happen to like him, there's a good chance he'll never call me back." They don't say why they ghost me, of course, but I have a few guesses. I'm passionate about monsters, and talk about my job a lot. I travel frequently, which makes it hard to have a carry on a stable relationship anyway. The few I've had usually fizzle and burn out.

He frowns in confusion. "Rena pretty," he says. "Why no mate?"

I laugh. Even by human standards I'm pretty average or below-average, and I've got a little extra junk in my trunk. Not really the pick of the litter at a bar. "For starters, I'm not pretty," I say. Maybe if I were a little more easygoing, my personality would be enough.

Morak shakes his head. "Wrong."

I quirk an eyebrow. Am I being told by a yeti that I'm nice to look at?

"Wrong?" I echo. "How would you know?"

"I know."

Finally, Morak releases my hand, and I find that slowly the color has crept back into it. He returns to my other hand which is still as cold as ice, like the rest of my body. This conversation has distracted me from it so far, but I'm starting to get weary again.

He says nothing else as he repositions himself on the floor. My eyelids are starting to flutter closed. "Awake!" Morak snaps, and I quickly jolt back to consciousness. "No sleep."

I groan. "But I'm so cold, and I'm so tired. Please, I just need to rest my eyes for a while." My chest, my thighs, every part of me is freezing. I want to escape it.

With a heavy sigh, Morak leans down towards me, and I feel one of his arms slip underneath my body. I wriggle against him. "I'm perfectly comfortable on this soft fur on the floor, thank you very much, and it's about time I went to bed!"

But he doesn't answer. He simply slides me towards him, then lies down on the fur. His other hand wraps around my waist, and though I'm still objecting, he's stronger than I am.

"Stop," he growls, and instinctually, I listen. "Cold. Need warm." His big hands bring me against his chest, so my face is buried in his white fur.

Oh, is it soft. He's soft and warm and strangely, he smells wonderful, like a Christmas tree. No, no, it's like lying in front of the fireplace, next to a Christmas tree. Yes, that's it. I breathe in a deep whiff of him, and it's as if my muscles all loosen at once. The heat of him around me makes my skin hurt, but in that way where you know the medicine is working.

"Wow," I mutter against his chest. "You're really warm."

"Yes," Morak answers. There's less annoyance in his voice now. "Warm good."

I nod in agreement. He's twice as soft as the fur on the ground is, and underneath it I can feel tough muscle, sturdy and solid. His arms are thick and his hands are huge. I move around a little to get more comfortable, and Morak grunts.

"Stop," he says.

"Sorry," I say. But I'm cold and my clothes are wet, and everything hurts.

Growling, Morak releases me and sits up. Before I can blink he's trying to pull apart the zipper of my jacket.

"Off," he says.

"What?" I clutch the wet jacket. "Why?"

"Cold!" Clearly, he has very little patience for me. "Off."

I need him if I'm not going to freeze to death so I do as I'm told, unzipping the big, heavy jacket, and he shoves it aside. But he's still not satisfied. He nods at my clothed body again. "Off."

I realize what he wants. It's like something out of a movie, where we have to cuddle naked to stay warm. But Morak hasn't seen a rom-com, so if he thinks this is the way I survive this, then I'll do it.

I manage to unbutton my shirt and squeeze the wet sleeves off, but my fingers are too cold for the pants. Without much preamble, Morak reaches down and tears open the mechanism, then slowly drags the wet slacks down my thighs and calves. Underneath I'm totally naked except for my bra and under-wear. He frowns at these objects, not sure what to make of them.

I'm not going to part with those. "No," I say, covering my chest.

He gets just the hint of a smile on his face, then nods. "Come." He lies back down and gestures for me to get close again. This time, his soft fur is everywhere and oh my god, does it feel good on my bare skin. Strangely, I start shivering, and I think that means my blood is starting to move again.

Then the itching starts. I move my arms, trying to scratch, but Morak lets out a warning sound and keeps me close.

"Stop," he says again.

"Sorry! But my skin itches all over." I can't help it. It feels like there are ants crawling everywhere. "I'm so fucking cold."

Morak growls, so I try to stop. That's when I feel something slowly growing against my thigh, thick and warm and definitely *not* covered in fur. I only have to wonder for a brief second before it occurs to me what it is.

Crap. I didn't mean to make him horny. But he doesn't move to do anything with it, and after a while, I'm able to ignore it.

Still, I wonder what it looks like down there. The skin of his hands is a leathery pink-brown; perhaps his cock would be the same color.

God. I have to stop. I know that it's been a long time since I had a date end by "going upstairs for coffee," but it can't have been *that* long. An employee at the Menagerie has already gotten in trouble for hooking up with a monster—not one, but two—and I'm not going to follow down that path and lose my job.

Soon my skin stops that infernal burning. I'm still cold to the bone, but my chattering has slowed. I don't notice when I fall asleep.

When I wake up a while later, Morak's breathing is steady. His arms are still wrapped tight around me, holding me close to his body, sharing his incredible heat. I've never felt so cozy in my life. I could probably sleep like this forever.

Eventually, though, I need to go pee. Now that my body has woken up, other parts of me are awake now, too. Gently I shake Morak's chest.

"Hey."

He groans, his arms tightening around me. He snuffles my head and sighs, then seems to suddenly realize who I am and where we are.

He sits up, lifting an arm to rub his eyes which leaves me unfortunately mostly naked and cold.

"Pee?" I ask. "Somewhere I can go to the bathroom, please?"

He sighs. Together, we manage to get me up to my feet, and Morak wraps an arm around me to hold me upright as he leads me towards the mouth of the cave, where it looks like only a white void is waiting for us.

The snow has piled up high already, and more of it is coming down in a thick curtain. Shit. This is an honest-to-god blizzard, and I'm stuck out here in it for who knows how long.

Morak clears away a chunk of snow with one arm, making a little alcove for me. He points at it. "Go."

What? With him standing right there?

"Turn around!" I say. Rolling his eyes, he turns around. I almost fall over when he releases me, but I manage to limp over into the snow, then pop a squat.

When I'm done, I wash off my hands in the snow and limp back inside the cave. He guides me over to the pelt, and there he bundles me up tight again. This time he rests his chin on the top of my head, and I find that my arms have found their way around his big chest. It's nice to be this near to someone and embrace them, even if he's only doing it so I don't die of frostbite.

After a while, I feel that thick object starting to nudge at my naked thigh once more. This time it sends a spark through me, straight up to the little nerve center right between my legs.

That's just great. Now he's turned on and so am I. By what? A huge yeti dick?

Oof. The thought barrels into me at full speed, and that pool of liquid lava is growing. He's big, I can tell that just from how it's touching me.

I feel like this should all be very awkward, but instead the air is charged with electricity. My heart is racing as more of my blood pumps downward.

I really want to know what that cock looks like, maybe even, what it feels like.

For science.

"Morak?" I ask quietly.

"Yes, Rena."

His voice sends a little shiver through me. "Are you, um... I mean, do you..." I have no idea how to say what I'm thinking. For once, words have failed me. "Can I, I mean..." I run a hand down his chest, towards his abdomen. He flexes very suddenly, and his arms around me tense up. "Sorry," I say, halting my movement. "I just, it's interesting, and I wanted to know if I could maybe..."

"Touch?" he interrupts. Thank god. It's as if he can read my mind. I nod quickly. He hums, and I'd almost say there's amusement in his voice as he says, "Yes. Rena touch."

His hips slide toward me almost imperceptibly, and I can suddenly feel the entire length of his big cock on my thigh. Holy fuck.

My curious hands travel down further between us, over his groin where the fur thins out. There, under my fingers, is a big, thick, leathery object that immediately twitches under my touch.

Morak lets out the smallest gasp. He must be sensitive. With care I bring my hand down the length of him, trying not to apply too much pressure until I get a lay of the land.

This is a once-in-a-lifetime opportunity, to be up close and personal with a monster like Morak. Not to mention that he's warm, soft, and incredibly well-endowed. Plus, he saved me from a snowstorm, and that makes me like him immensely, despite the fact I was only out there because I was chasing after him.

When I reach his cockhead, I find a droplet of pre-come already there. I must really turn him on, I think. That's gratifying.

I run my hands up and down, just feeling him and testing different pressures to see what he likes. I don't get much data out of it, though, because it seems Morak enjoys just about everything I'm doing. The longer I stroke him, the more his hips start to move under my touch, and his arms are tightening around me.

Suddenly, his hands fall down to mine, and he pulls them away.

"Shit," I say, curling up. "I'm sorry, did I—?"

Fervently he shakes his head. "Good," he says. "Too much good." He's breathing heavier now, and his dick is pretty firmly pressed against my belly.

"Is that bad?" I ask.

Morak exhales sharply. He seems to regain control of himself, and then his hand starts to move down my back. "I touch," he finally says. "I touch Rena, yes?"

Oh. I see. He wants to get me in on the action. I'm definitely not going to object to that.

"Yes, it's okay to touch."

With a nod, his hand ventures further down, over the round peaks of my butt. Curious about them, he stops to examine, and his cock pulses against me as he squeezes each cheek.

That's hot in a way I can't really explain.

Now his other hand is moving, finding its way between us, past where his cock is leaving wet trails on my skin. It stops as it reaches the hair between my legs, and investigates it for a moment before descending further down.

His hands might be as big as plates, but they're soft as he brushes over the outside of my sex, just a feather touch. He explores more, dipping one finger between my folds, where he must feel how wet I am already. All that rubbing of his huge cock got me good and fired up.

"Mmm," Morak breathes as he tests more of me, noting each of my labia, then the slit further down. As he drags his hand back up, the pad of his finger passes over my clit and I let out a small gasp. He pauses, then repeats the motion. This time, I moan. I can hear his heartbeat speed up as he returns to the place that triggered my reaction and starts to play more earnestly there, flicking it back and forth, rubbing it, and trying out all the different ways to make me tremble and groan.

"Inside," I murmur into his chest. "Put it inside."

He pauses, then seems to understand what I'm asking for and slides his finger down lower. When he finds me, I'm so soaked that it glides in easily.

"Oh!" I clench his arms in my hands, and I can see him grinning from the corner of my eye. He experiments some more, thrusting the finger in and out, curling it and stroking me, measuring each of my responses. When he brings his thumb up to touch my tender nub, I nuzzle into his shoulder and moan. There's a rumble of amusement in his chest.

Now he's gotten me all stirred up and I want more. That thick cock is still drizzling come down my belly, and I can't stop thinking about it or how it might feel. I wonder if he would even want that.

I guess there's no way to know unless you ask.

While he plays with me, I bring my hands back to his length, and start to stroke it. Morak pauses his assault, and leans back so he can look down at me. There's a wide, questioning look in his eyes.

"Do you want to?" I ask. "Have sex?"

His hand stills, and slowly he withdraws it. I think he's about to turn me away, but then he peers at my face with those bright, golden eyes and nods his head.

"I want."

He grips me by the hips and, without much preamble, rolls me over onto my side so I'm facing away from him. I'm surprised by this, but I don't object. Perhaps this is the way yetis mate? He reaches down again, sliding his hand between my ass cheeks and around to my slick pussy. He positions himself behind me and presses his cock down to slide between my legs. I think he's about to just dive in, which I wouldn't mind, but instead he runs the thick head of his cock back and forth along my hot center, slathering himself up with my juices and his. He's breathing faster now and so am I, anticipating whatever comes next. His other hand runs up and down my back as he lowers his hips.

When he presses at my entrance, he's bigger than I expected. Luckily, his finger-fucking lubed me up well, and with one sharp thrust he's inside me.

I cry out, not expecting so much so fast, but god, does Morak feel good. He doesn't go deep, though, and gives me a moment to adjust, pulling in and out shallowly. I clench the fur under us in my hands as he opens me up.

"Feels good," he groans behind me, his fingers squeezing my ass as he ventures further in. I'm tight around that thick cock, so tight, and I can feel every movement exquisitely. He continues thrusting at his slow pace, sliding deeper each time and urging me wider for him.

Holy shit. We've only just started and this might very well be the best fuck I've ever had.

I lean forward so I can take in even more of him, and

behind me, Morak growls in pleasure. Soon he's buried in me up to the hilt, his heavy sac slapping my ass with each stroke, his leathery hands gripping my hips. I'm trembling all over as his thick length slicks in and out, pushing me ever higher.

"Up," Morak grunts in a commanding voice. He grabs onto my waist and, still lodged deep inside me, lifts me onto my knees. He leans forward so his soft fur hugs my body, and takes a powerful whiff of my hair. He lets out a pleased grumble, and his hands reach around to my breasts so he's fully ensconcing me. His hands run over my bra, then he shoves it out of the way so he can reach my nipples.

"Beautiful," he murmurs, plucking them. "Delicious."

Then he starts to move inside me again, his hands taking in the curve of my hip, the thick flesh of my thighs, the roundness of my belly. One hand ducks down between my legs and starts to rub over my clit. Almost immediately I'm soaring, my body twitching and shaking under his tender attacks. I'm so close to the sun that I'm crying out. Morak starts to pound into me faster, that huge cock spreading me even further, reaching a place deep down inside me that's never been touched before.

"Fuck," I moan, my arms giving out underneath me so my ass is sticking up in the air. He doesn't slow his pace, and my butt bounces on his furry belly with every thrust. Now he's grunting and groaning too, and somehow swelling up even more as he grips me hard with both hands. My climax hits me like a train. I scream when he barrels through it, plunging into me even as my pussy clamps down. I'm spinning even higher, and I can hear Morak roaring as he releases. There's so much of him that it spills out down my thighs, and still he pumps more. A second orgasm strikes out of nowhere, like a stray thunderbolt, and my whole body collapses underneath him.

Panting, Morak crouches over me and runs his fingers through my hair.

"Rena," he says quietly, running soothing hands down my back. "Good."

I nod in agreement. "Good."

As he withdraws even more of his come slips out and drizzles down my leg. Wow. Who knew that yetis came like waterfalls?

While I lie there feeling like a marionette with cut strings, Morak gathers me up in his arms and brings me close against his warm, plush body. When I bury my face in the hair of his chest, I wonder if just maybe, I'm glad I got lost in the snow.

The next morning, I wake up naked and sweating curled up in the curve of Morak's arm. The fire has died down, and he must have gotten up during the night to lay out my clothes to dry.

When he awakens too, he doesn't let me go. He mounts me again, clearly preferring this method of having sex, which I don't mind at all. He milks my orgasm out of me, nursing it with slow strokes until my cries are echoing around his cave and he's slamming through my tight channel, bringing me to a place I didn't think was possible.

When we're spent and all I want to do is go back to sleep again, Morak rolls me up in his embrace.

"I will come," he says.

"Again?" I ask. Then his words sink a little deeper in. "Wait, do you mean to the Menagerie? You'll come back with me?"

He just nods his big, hairy head. When I look up, there's a small smile on his wide face.

"Yes."

At least now he'll be safe from those men.

When the blizzard finally abates, he packs a few small belongings, including a knife, which I assure him he won't need, some stones for starting a fire, and a skin for heating up water. Then he produces an object I didn't expect: a comb. He brushes all of his hair so it's white and straight and shining and then nods at me.

"We go."

It's a long hike back to the house and partway through, Morak picks me up and carries me against his chest because I'm too slow and too cold in my little booties.

Finally we reach the house again, and one of the men storms out carrying his gun. I run up with my hands in the air.

"Wait, wait," I call out. "It's fine. We're going. Okay?"

He jerks the barrel of the gun towards my car. "We dug it out for you," he grumbles.

"Thanks."

It's a challenge getting Morak's big body into the car, an object which he regards with a deep suspicion. I can't imagine how he's going to handle airplanes, but he seems to trust me now. I assure him that where we're going, he'll never have to worry about guns or cars or airplanes again.

"Rena is there?" he asks, more than once.

"Yes. I'll be there." I don't know what that entails, but I'll figure it out. Maybe I'll try to get that rule changed.

"Good." Morak settles into the leather seat, making himself comfortable. "I like Rena."

"Yeah," I say, putting the car in drive. "I like you, too."

The Deep Dive

THEY TRIED TO TELL ME DEEP-SEA DIVING WAS DANGEROUS. MY equipment could fail and then the pressure would kill me. I might make a mistake down there, stay submerged for too long and not be able to make it back up again.

All of this is my parents, of course. I've always been an explorer, a risk-taker, a daredevil, and it drives them nuts. As much as I tell them that I've practiced, that I know what I'm doing, they still won't believe me. Which, I have to admit, I understand. As a child I broke plenty of bones diving from high branches and leaping into shallow lakes. It was a lot of money and many ER visits.

It's not that I think I'm indestructible. It's just that I want to explore everything, do everything, see everything, and experience everything the world has to offer me. That is the point of being alive after all, isn't it? I've been to the top of mountains and looked down upon the world, flown through the sky on parachutes and hang gliders, visited some of the most remote places on earth on snowmobiles and camels. There's always something new to discover on this planet, and I want to witness it with my own eyes.

The sea was a vast unknown to me, so naturally, I had to explore it. I started small, with snorkeling in Hawaii, then scuba diving in the Gulf. I practiced and practiced, working seasonal jobs in-between to save up for the big expedition.

It's a wondrous place, the ocean, and also delightfully terrifying. We are helpless beneath the waves, at the mercy of sharks and jellyfish and whatever other predatory unknowns. It's exciting to imagine what kinds of marvels I might see at the bottom.

I hired out on a fishing boat over the summer to get a feel for life on the ocean. I made friends with some local tour guides, and with one of them even climbed into bed. That's one of the other perks of traveling: There are many interesting people to meet and all sorts of bodies to explore. I once went with a pair of best friends to the Himalayas, and a few days into our trip we got curious about each other. I've participated in dozens of interesting sexual situations before, but it was my first time taking two cocks at once. They filled me up in a way I've never been filled before, and by the end of the trip, there was come practically leaking out of my pores. Yet another wondrous new experience to add to my collection.

Eventually, the tour guides suggested taking me out with them on a dive, free of charge. The boat will carry us far from the coast to a nearby reef, and then we'll swim to the bottom there. Everyone dives together, but we're free to explore a little on our own as long as we keep an eye on our oxygen.

We get suited up, me and the tourists and one of the guides, and prepare. I put on a suit, a helmet, and an oxygen tank, and ready myself for the immense pressure we'll face as we go deeper. Then we're off the side of the ship and steadily sinking to the bottom.

The reef comes into view, and its beauty is unparalleled. Thousands of fish swarm the strange, colorful plants that grow there, fleeing as we land. I investigate all the different types of coral, and even spot a bright orange octopus hiding under a rock. He's so cute that I just want to hug him, but I leave him be so I don't frighten him.

Unfortunately the other tourists are disturbing the wildlife, so I make a point of finding a different area of the reef to explore on my own. The sea floor slopes down here, descending into darkness. The light on my helmet only reaches a few dozen feet in front of me—I could encounter anything here and probably not see it until it was on top of me. My nerves are alight at the idea of being surprised, of witnessing something unique and unusual and perhaps even dangerous.

"Don't go too far, Emma," one of my tour guide friends had said. We were still tethered to the boat, of course, but we had a lot of leeway. "You never know what you might find down there."

Still, I'm drawn deeper and deeper, curious where this sea shelf goes.

Suddenly, a shadow passes through the light cast by my lamp. It's larger than a fish, and while one part of me hopes it isn't a shark, another part of me hopes it is.

But the shadow is gone as quickly as it appeared. Perhaps I've scared it off, whatever it was, and I feel a stab of disappointment. I wonder what sort of creature it was.

The line is starting to lose slack, so I suppose I should turn around. My oxygen levels are fine, but it will take me some time to work my way back to the rest of the group, so I turn around and start back up the slope toward the reef.

That's when I feel a tug. Curious, I glance up at my tether, and find it has been pulled far to one side. I swing my light around, looking for whatever has grabbed hold of it. Perhaps it got caught on a coral, or some large bundle of algae floating around.

There's another tug, even stronger. Once more that shadow passes in front of my light, and this time, I get a better glimpse of it. It's big, whatever it is—about the size of a human, and it has a huge, thick tail. Perhaps a shark has glommed onto my line and decided to try and take it.

I yank on the tether as I head up the slope, trying to free it. But the pressure only grows. Whatever has grabbed hold of me is much stronger than I am.

The shape comes into view again, and this time, it isn't moving so quickly. I make out a large body with what looks like a head and two arms. The rest is a tail, almost as long as I am, with two great fins on the end. Whatever it is, it's carrying my line and trying to drag me down the shelf into the dark oblivion.

Fuck. I'm so done for.

I pull on the cable, fighting the pressure. The creature comes closer, edging into the bright view of my headlamp. It is most certainly no fish, and not a shark or a squid, either. It's flailing, massive tail is whipping around and dragging me along with it.

Wait. It doesn't have a hold of me. It's tangled in my tether, and it's trying to get out.

"Stop!" I call out, but my voice is muffled by my helmet and by the water. I push off the sea floor and start swimming towards it, and scales flash as my light hits them. The closer I get, the clearer the creature becomes. It has a humanoid head and shoulders, but the lower body is trapped in my line. When I'm nearly close enough to touch it, the whole creature finally comes clearly into view.

It's no animal. Panicked eyes with nearly white irises stare back at me, and long arms with strong hands are trying to unwind my tether from the place on its body where it should have legs. Instead, the powerful chest and strong abdomen widen into a thick, long tail, with two fins along the hips. The scaled tail is bigger than the man's upper body, and looks to be seven or eight feet long. Whatever this creature-person is, he can't get a grip enough to unwind the tether, and the rapid flapping of his tail is only tying us tighter and tighter together.

Then, suddenly, the cord to the ship breaks.

Fuck. Now we're floating loose, and only this monster and I are connected. I pull on the line to drag myself closer. The only way I'll survive this is if I can free myself and then swim back to the surface, and hope the boat finds me. That involves getting the cable off of this thrashing, bizarre body.

When I'm near enough to touch the him, massive hands reach out to push me away. They have five fingers, with webbing in between.

"Please!" I hope I'm close enough that he can hear me through the helmet. "Let me help!"

The hands gripping me soften, and I look up to find a surprisingly human face staring down at me.

Oh, wow. He's beautiful and otherworldly, with white-blue eyes and long, white lashes. He even has white eyebrows. Most of his hair is pulled back into a braid, and if we weren't underwater, I would think he's some sort of alien. There are fins where I would expect ears to be, and gills pulse along his throat.

It's a fucking mermaid. Mer-*man*, I suppose. As if the details matter right now while I'm being tossed around by my tether like a cat toy. I reach for where it's wrapped around his huge, finned lower body, and try to get my fingers under the thick cord.

The creature very suddenly falls still. There's a heavy object underneath his flesh—no, two of them: Two big lumps just above where the tether is tightening around him, cutting into his scales.

Maybe he can't understand me, I think. I need to convince him that I can help him. I try to be gentle as I loosen the line, but he starts to thrash again. My hands rub the lumps over and over as I hold on, searching out the loose end so I can hopefully pull it free. Finally I find it. I grab the torn cable and start to unwind it from his body, and it seems he finally understands what I'm trying to do. He relaxes just long enough for me to unspool one layer of the tether, but he flailed so much that it's now wound around at least three times. When I reach the second loop, though, his hands abruptly grab onto my wrists, stopping their movement. He's staring down at me, those intense pale eyes drawn down into an intense glare.

"I'm just trying to help," I say, hoping he can hear me and understand me. That's when I see that those two lumps underneath his scales are turning into something else. The scales are parting, revealing two slits, and something is starting to emerge from them.

Suddenly the creature seizes me in his arms, pressing me hard and tight against his body. I let out a scream that's swallowed up by the helmet. His massive tail moves in the water, beating it once, and then twice, which propels us forward like I'm tied to a rocket.

"Let me go!" I cry out, but the creature ignores me, keeping me locked tight against his chest no matter how hard I fight. He's sculpted, I'll give him that. His dense, carved pecs are all I can see as I'm dragged along.

After a few panicked minutes of fighting, I realize that there's no way I'm going to escape his powerful arms without breaking my connection to my oxygen tank. Where is he taking me? Unfortunately, I have no choice but to wait and find out.

Everything around me turns dark as we dip into what looks like a huge cavern. I wonder how far we are from the boat now, because I didn't see any caves during my trek along the sea floor. Soon I'm blind as the last of the light from above the ocean's surface vanishes, and all I can see is the pale flesh of the merman's chest under my bright headlamp.

This is the first time that I wonder if I'll die. Eventually my oxygen will run out, and I'll be far, far below the surface, inside some cave with no way out.

Then, suddenly, there's light again. It isn't sunlight, though. It's vaguely greenish, but I can't get a good look from my vantage point. We've slowed down, I can tell that much, and the merman is starting to loosen his iron hold on me.

I try to push away using all the force in my hands to shove against his toned chest. But the cord is still attached to him, and I can't get very far before he grabs my wrist and yanks me back in. His huge tail thrashes one more time, hard, and then we break through the surface of the water.

What? The surface? Abruptly the merman releases me, and I tumble backwards onto hard stone. Now I can see, and I stop moving completely as I take in our surroundings.

We're inside a cave still, that much is clear. The light is coming from all around us, emanating out from tiny blobs covering the walls and ceiling.

Bio-luminescence. I've seen it before, late at night in Costa Rica. But never have I witnessed it in such great quantities. The tiny blobs are pulsing, letting out light with each breath, and right in front of me is the man who kidnapped me.

Merman, I correct myself. He's freakishly pale, the surface of his skin almost translucent. He's only a few feet away, floating in the water that laps against the rock where I'm sitting. Where a man's waist would usually become hips, this creature has dark blue scales that shine under the bioluminescent light, wide fins flaring out from the sides. We're still tied together by the tether, so I can't roll away from him like all my instincts are demanding.

The merman doesn't move as he studies me with those bright, strange eyes. Maybe now I can talk to him and convince him to let me go. I reach for the helmet of my scuba suit and unclasp it, gasping as it finally pulls free of my head. It clatters to the stone.

"Please," I say. "Let me go. I won't do anything. I won't hurt you. Just please—"

He interrupts me. "*Passssssh*." His full lips whisper out a word I don't recognize. The merman gestures at the cable wrapped around his long tail, then waves a hand at me, urging me forward. Some more words come out, words that are musical and strange and don't resemble any human language that I know, but I think I understand his meaning.

He wants me to untie him. That must be why he brought me here. *All right, Emma. You can do this.* I crawl forward into the water, reaching again for his waist. He grunts and shifts, moving his hips closer to me so I can access the cable. Uneasily I slide my fingers under it and start to pull. Again I feel those two strange lumps, where a groin would be if he had legs instead of a tail, and I can't help brushing over them as the tether slowly comes loose. And again, two slits appear between his scales, widening and opening like gills. Once I've worked another layer of tether free, there are two thick, rounded objects starting to come out. The merman grunts again, and this time the sound is deeper, more guttural.

Finally, I unwind the last loop and the cable binding us together falls free. I gasp with relief, now finally released from him. Those two odd protrusions have extended even further, and that's the moment that I realize what they are: Two big, fleshy cocks.

I let out a shocked whimper. I've accidentally aroused him by removing the tether, and this is the result. But they are strangely mesmerizing as they get bigger and thicker, and pink heads emerge from the flesh at the tips. They have an aerodynamic shape to them, and against all logical, mental, or emotional sense, I imagine what one would feel like inside me.

Whoa. I scuttle backwards on the stone, letting out a panicked breath. But the merman is unmoving, his arms crossed over his chest. He says something else in that language

I can't understand, and swims closer to the edge of the water, holding the cable in his hands. Is he going to tie me up with them?

He gestures at the cables and says something again, nodding at me. Then his face shifts into a smile, encouraging and friendly, like I'm a child.

I think he's thanking me.

"No big deal," I say, raising my hands up in surrender. "I'm glad we got it worked out. But can you take me back now?"

He tilts his head, sensing I'm asking a question. I point over our heads. "Back to the surface," I say. "I need to go home." With a sigh, he makes a wavy motion with his hand, then points down at my feet and shakes his head. Right, I don't have a big tail like him, that's true, and my flippers won't help guide me through the dark. I'll need his help to get back out of here.

I point at him. "Take me up." I wrap my arms around myself, then make the same wavy gesture. Again I motion towards where the sky would be if we weren't underwater.

The merman rubs his gills, then quirks an eyebrow at me. No, I don't have gills, either. Maybe he thought I was drowning.

His cocks are even larger now, fully engorged with blood. I wonder if perhaps I'm here because he wants to use them. Is that it?

He catches me staring and raises an eyebrow. The smile on his face spreads as he raises a single finger and beckons me towards him.

There's no way. This is absurd. I'm not going to fuck a fishman I found at the bottom of the sea. My body, though, has completely different ideas. There's a familiar heat gathering right between my legs, and I squeeze them together to try to squash it.

Again, he beckons me, and this time I think a little more seriously about it. He is my way out of here, after all.

Unbidden I remember that night in the Himalayas and an

empty place inside me squeezes tight. God, I'm getting all wet inside my scuba suit over a very ripped guy with a mermaid tail.

And two dicks. Don't forget the two dicks, Emma.

It's not like anyone can see me. It's not like anyone would know if I did. Anyway, nobody would believe it if I told them—merpeople don't exist. We all know that.

I can't believe I'm starting to think in concrete terms about this, but I am and it's taking over all my rational thought. Those heavy, swollen cocks, and the perfect, carved body; the handsome face with high cheekbones and a powerful, square jaw.

Fuck. What's stopping me besides me? Well, not to mention the huge tail instead of legs, and don't forget, the two dicks. I have no idea how merpeople have sex. It looks pretty similar, though. Do females have two vaginas? Or are they intended to take two at a—

The merman scatters my thoughts by reaching down with one hand to stroke his left cock. He squeezes it, hard, and a droplet of pre-come emerges at the tip. His eyes are riveted to me, and his eyelids have drooped ever-so-slightly. He knows I'm considering his offer.

Oh, damn. I'm going to do it, aren't I?

I creep towards him, and he nods encouragingly. Then he takes his other cock in hand and strokes it, too. Instantly I imagine how full he could stuff me with them, and I wiggle a little closer. He releases himself and leans forward, extending one arm slowly so he doesn't startle me. He rests his hand on my cheek, and without meaning to I lean into it. He draws the hand down to my neck, where he tugs at the collar of my scuba suit.

He wants me to take it off. He's fully naked already—by default, I suppose—and I should probably do the same.

I climb up to my feet and reach for the zipper on the back of the suit, then tug it down in the least-sexy way I could possibly imagine. I have to wriggle, the thick fabric clinging to my arms and legs as I try to pull it off.

Once I'm fully disrobed, he beckons me again. I'm like a marionette on a string as I walk towards him, stopping just inches away so his face is level with my pelvis. With surprising gentleness he reaches out and runs that same smooth, pale hand from my belly down to my curls. He has a curious look on his face as he slides his hand between my legs, and my thighs part just enough that he can get through.

His mouth forms an O-shape as he reaches my center, which is already dewy with my arousal. He searches through my folds with one finger, skating over my clit, which makes me twitch and gasp. With a tilt of his head he does it again, and again I shiver. His fascination grows as he explores lower, and his finger finds my wet slit. Without much preamble he slips it inside me and my pussy happily welcomes him in. Oh, that's good.

Suddenly he withdraws his hand, and I let out a whimper. The merman drifts backwards in the water, then gestures for me to follow. Uncertain, I approach the edge of the stone shelf and drop my legs in. I'm rewarded with a nod of approval. Once more he swims closer, and reaches under my butt to tug me all the way forward. I don't fight his rough handling or even mind it. I have a feeling I'm going to enjoy the sort of lover he seems to be.

Taking each of my knees in a hand, he pulls my thighs apart, and I let him. With our heads and torsos at a much more even level now, I realize that he's big, bigger than a human at least. Again his hand finds that moist place between my legs. He repeats the motion over my clit, and I gasp. He seems pleased with this reaction and continues it, increasing his speed little by little, until I'm moaning under his fingers. I realize that his other hand is busy, too, stroking one of his cocks while he plays with me. There's a sly look on his face as the pitch of my voice climbs. I'm getting a hand job from a merman, and it's amazing. He's pinpointing every motion that makes me tremble and repeating it until I'm moaning and shivering and inches away from my orgasm. His wide smile has faded into something more determined and predatory. He's stroking himself faster and harder now, eyes pinned on mine as he takes me right over the edge, into oblivion.

My cry catches in my throat and I'm silent as it takes me. I fall back onto the stone floor, shaking with the force of my climax.

A shadow appears over me. My merman has slid up the stone, and now supports himself above me with one arm. His finned tail slaps the water, pushing him closer. He's stroking his other cock now, and they're both dripping.

My pussy clenches just watching him. Those strange, ice-blue eyes are studying mine, and he hovers, waiting for me to give the word.

I'm about to get fucked in a freaky stone cavern by a merman. Of all the experiences possible on planet Earth, I'm about to partake in the most unlikely and incredible one.

I reach down to the gap between my thighs and and pull apart my lower lips, then lift my hips towards his. A sinful look comes over him, and he guides one of his huge, gently-sloped cocks right to my waiting entrance.

He's slick with his own juices and mine, and perfectly shaped for simply slipping inside. That smooth fuselage widens me as the head slides deeper, and I jerk at the abrupt rush of pleasure it sends through me. My back arches up and I cry out, my voice filling the small cavern.

Oh, merman cock is good. Very good.

He doesn't ram in hard like I expected, but takes his time thrusting in deeper, and then letting me adjust, and then going deeper still. It feels like there's no limit to him. His other cock drags against my thigh with every stroke. He takes my hand and guides it downward to the space between us, and wraps my fingers around the other soft head.

This is insane. I'm giving him a hand job while also taking him as thoroughly as my body will allow, and it's probably the best feeling in the world. Soon I'm eagerly swallowing him up, moaning and throwing my head back as he starts to speed up inside me, my hand gripping his other pliable cock and pumping it in tempo with his thrusts.

Then, suddenly, he stops. He slides me down into the water a little deeper, so my ass is floating with his surprisingly squishy, soft cock buried deep. I love the texture of him, how it conforms perfectly to my body, filling every inch. He reaches down beneath me, exploring me. He seems concerned when he doesn't find what he's looking for.

"I don't have a second vagina," I try to explain to him. He tilts his head, perplexed. His hand ventures further, and when he comes across the puckered hole between my cheeks, he grins at me. "That's not what you think it is," I say, but he's already testing the edges of me, trying to fit a finger inside me.

Oh, god. He wiggles just the pad, squeezing it in a tiny bit at a time, teasing me open. Once the pad is inside, he's suddenly buried in my ass up to the knuckle. His finger in combination with his amazing fish cock feels like gold and sparkles and magic. He starts to thrust with both at the same time and immediately I'm lost, writhing and moaning and bucking my hips to meet his. Looking into his eyes is wildly erotic because they never stray from mine, intense and emotional and deeply intelligent. I easily rise up to meet my next orgasm, and I can feel his fleshy cock squeezing in and out of me as my channel seizes up around him. For a moment he breaks eye contact, because his eyes are rolling back into his head in pleasure. I'm boneless, nearly deflated, and slowly he removes his finger. He continues that slow, flawless motion with his cock inside me, waiting for me to recover.

Again he tugs me deeper into the water, and strangely, starts to turn me to one side. I don't understand what's happening at first—my mind is too foggy with bliss to really object to being manhandled—until I feel a familiar soft, coned head prodding at my ass.

Oh. He wants to use it. And he wants to use it *there*.

I'm not prepared the way I was in the Himalayas. The three of us worked at it for a few days, the two of them taking turns in my pussy until I was ready to have them at the same time. When my tight little hole struggles to widen for him, my merman stops and looks at me with concern. He's confused as to why this one isn't behaving like the other one.

But I'm not going to pass up the opportunity to get double-dicked-down by an otherworldly merman I found on a deep sea diving trip. He guides his second cock back to my pussy, where he's already fit one, and starts to try to fit the second one inside.

Oh, that's not going to work.

I stop him with one hand, then completely twist sideways so my full array of tools are exposed to him. Thank god we're in the water, where such a position is even possible. I'm still halfway up the rock, and his tail keeps most of our bodies above the surface, the sea simply allowing me to hold my hips wherever I want.

I reach down and spread my cheeks wide, and bring one of his hands down to my puckered hole to encourage him to keep playing with me. Obediently he slides one finger back inside, and I almost come all over him again. He thrusts it, drawing it in a circle to spread and open me. I close my eyes and nearly go flat on the rock, overcome by how god damned good he feels.

And then suddenly, there are two fingers. I gasp and clench, and the cock that's inside me is nearly ejected by the force of it. My merman groans and sinks both his fingers inside me, and I'm almost to the edge of a cliff with no bottom on the other side. He fucks me even harder, his hand pumping me while his cock stuffs me full. I'm almost over the edge, crying out and dragging my fingers across the rock when he, much to my distress, slows down. Withdrawing his fingers, he reaches up to his mouth to spit a gratuitous amount of saliva onto them. He guides it back down to my tight hole, spreading it all over.

There's no way he'd be able to do this underwater, I think. So how do the merpeople usually do it? I wonder if that's what this cave is for, having sex. Is this his personal sex cave? Has he had sex with other humans or merpeople in here?

I can't think about it any longer because now he's nudging the head of his incredible second cock inside my ass. This entrance, though, is much less forgiving. He's patient, testing each depth as he wedges more and more of that huge, spongey, aerodynamic cock through. It starts to put so much pressure on my pussy—his other cock already filling it full—that I'm moaning and whimpering and clutching the stone even though there's nothing to grab onto, because the sensation is so intense I think I might pop.

Slowly, ever-so-slowly, he starts to move again. Now each cock is traveling in tandem, easy and exploratory, and my body is rioting because I haven't ever taken something that big inside me, not to mention *two* of said big somethings. Every single thrust makes an obscene sound because I'm wet as a faucet and stretched as tight as I can possibly be. Still, those slick cocks slide in and out of me in perfect synchronicity, and soon I'm crying out and moaning and sobbing all at once as my body is stormed by intense, blinding pleasure. I almost can't bear it.

My merman mutters something guttural, and his webbed hands clutch my thighs even tighter. He fucks me harder, faster, and every single muscle in my body is taut as a rubber band. I'm screaming now because it's the only thing I can do as those incredible cocks squelch and squeeze and squish inside me. A tsunami starts to bear down on me and I worry that when it finally strikes, I might simply be crushed underneath it and cease to exist. His eyes are closed and his head is thrown back, his perfect abdominals flexing with every thorough, plundering thrust. As I clench tighter and tighter around him, he starts saying something in his own language that sounds almost like a prayer. One of his hands squeezes my ass while the other dips down to where his cock is spreading my pussy as wide as it can possibly go, and he starts to investigate my clit.

Oh. I'm done.

I scream as my climax thunders through me, flattening me, and both my holes clamp down. My merman groans a string of words, slamming into me now, inflating my orgasm larger with each thrust. It consumes me, turns me inside-out, and I'm coming so hard that liquid is bursting out of me with each stroke of his cock. He tenses up and his shoulders curl down as he crouches over me like he's protecting me with his body. Just when I don't think I can take any more, he roars, and he shoves himself fully in. His pale eyes are wide, mouth open as he pumps a half-dozen more times, gushing into both of my holes. It streams out of me, down my thighs, over the fat swell of his cocks where I'm clamped tight around them.

We lie like that, gasping, me on my side on the rock and him holding himself up with his elbows, bracketing my head between them. He brushes his forehead against mine, and I think they must not have kissing in merpeople culture. I turn my shoulders and plant a kiss on his cheek anyway, and he exhales with surprise. Then a smile takes over his face, and he does the same back to me—it's sloppy, but adorable.

Eventually he withdraws himself and lies down next to me. As his two cocks soften, they are swallowed back up into those two slits at his groin, which close and disappear. He slides down into the water, stopping at the crux of my legs to leave a kiss on my swollen, slick pussy as well. He points upward, making the swimming gesture.

He's going to take me back.

My merman waits in the water as I drag myself to my feet, my legs unsteady underneath me, and start putting my scuba suit back on. Then I reattach the helmet and latch it into place, making sure my oxygen is working. Finally I slip on my flippers and awkwardly descend into the water. He's watching in amusement as I swim up to him, and he wraps an arm tightly around me. Then my face is pressed to his chest again and we dive under the water.

He takes me all the way up to the surface, his finlike ears moving from side to side as he searches for something. We swim on for a while until, up ahead, the boat comes into sight.

My merman turns me towards him and once more caresses the side of my face with his hand. Then he plants another sloppy kiss on my cheek and slides down under the waves.

"Hey!" I call out, waving my arms. Someone pops up on deck. "Over here!"

"Emma! You're alive!"

Everyone wants to know how I survived for so long and still had plenty of oxygen left. They had been looking for me for at more than an hour. I just shrug and call it good luck that I found my way back to them after the tether got cut on a sharp coral.

I will take my heavenly fuck with a merman to the grave.

Office Werewolf

RAVEN

I HAVE A SECRET.

It's just a little secret, roughly the size of a bullet. I carry a teeny remote around in my pocket so I can turn it off if I really need to pay attention in a meeting. Most of the time, though, I put it in and let it vibrate.

Maybe it makes me some kind of creep to come in to work with a vibe shoved up my pussy, but sometimes that's the only way I make it through the day. I broke up with my boyfriend, Amos, just a couple months ago. It was for the best—he was a real mama's boy, and there were some jealousy issues that had started to become control issues.

But damn, we had the best sex. Mind-blowing sex. The kind of sex where your eyes are about to roll out of your head and you think your body might simply combust. I miss that the most. I've always had a monster of a sex drive, and Amos could keep up with me. That's been hard to find in my life.

"Raven?" I jerk up when one of my coworkers says my

name. It's Connor, the guy who works a few cubicles behind me. He's a nice guy, if a little quiet. He doesn't speak up much during meetings, but every once in a while he'll save me a donut if I didn't make it to the break room on time, or handle one of my calls when I'm overloaded. He's tall, with perfectly bronze skin and black hair and a surprisingly wide set of shoulders. The epitome of tall, dark, and broody, which has always made him "off limits" in my mind. Guys like him are either only interested in a casual fling or messed up somewhere deep down.

Not to mention that we're co-workers.

"What's up?" I ask, trying to ignore the way my pussy clenches around the vibe lodged in it. It sends little ripples of pleasure straight up into my abdomen.

"I had a question about a customer," he says. "They said they talked to you and you gave them a price quote? A discounted one?"

Oh, right. They wanted to open a few accounts at once, so I'd gotten clearance from the boss to offer them a bulk discount.

"You can route the customer back to me, if you want," I tell him.

He stands there awkwardly for a moment, not responding. His nostrils flare, and his pupils have dilated to take up most of his iris.

"Um..." He fumbles around for the words he wants. "No, that's okay. You're probably busy. I just wanted to know the code you used for the discount."

I wonder what's made him so uneasy? I turn to my computer and pull up the customer account, then scribble down the code on a sticky note. I peel it off and hand it to him. "Here you go. Should still work."

Connor takes the sticky note quickly, trying not to let our hands touch. Huh. I wonder if his opinion of me has changed in the last few weeks. Maybe I said something or did something to turn the tides. I wouldn't be surprised. Sometimes my mouth runs away with me.

"Thanks," he says, and scoots off back to his cubicle.

That's too bad. I kind of liked Connor.

Once he's gone, I take out the remote and turn it up. It's easy to close my eyes and imagine him without a shirt as the bullet vibrates on.

CONNOR

Spring is the worst time of year. Not because I have allergies or anything. Honestly, I would take seasonal allergies any day over what I go through every March-through-goddamned-May. Living through mating season, with no pack and no mate, is hell on Earth.

Yeah, I got kicked out. It was a long time ago. I was young and rough and a little full of myself, and I challenged the alpha of our pack to a fight for dominance.

I still have the scars from getting beaten into a pulp.

What led me to do something so utterly moronic as challenging the pack leader, we may never know, but I was firmly booted out, and there aren't really any other werewolf packs in the tri-county area. So now I'm here, working at Samson Enterprises as a lackey sales guy, just another body in a cubicle tapping away at a keyboard and taking phone calls.

The worst part about working here, though, is Raven.

She's hot. Absolutely five-alarm, breath on fire, smoke-coming-out-of-your-ears hot. The worst part about her, besides being my dream girl, is that she also has sex leaking out of her pores. Literally.

I'm not sure what it is that she's doing all day, but in the last two weeks, the scent of her arousal has been all over. It's permeated every last corner of the office, a perfume that wafts around her as she goes to meetings, to other cubicles, or to the bathroom. On top of doing my job, I spend a not-so-insignificant amount of time trying to keep my boner down around her. I close my eyes, count to ten, and try to picture an old man's limp penis just so I can stand up and move around without it looking obvious that my cock is attempting to escape my pants.

Maybe, if it weren't the middle of April, I'd have an easier time of it. Unfortunately, with that smell everywhere, Raven is all I can think about. My body wants nothing more than to bend her over and pump her full of my cubs. I'll zone out in the middle of a customer call and miss half of what they're saying. In meetings I do everything I can not to stare at her, not to mention grab her and throw her against a wall and bury my cock in her.

Woof. The power that last thought has over me is monumental, and I spend most of my time trying to fight it back.

After I went and spoke to Raven about the discount code, I then had to put it into the computer while still talking on the phone, my dick begging desperately for my attention. Well, for her attention really, but my hand will just have to do.

Finally I put down the phone, thank god, and make my way to the office bathroom as quickly and discreetly as possible. Once I'm inside one of the stalls with my pants hiked down, I pull myself out of my boxers. I'm already dripping with pre-come, and quite a lot of it, at that. As I start to stroke myself, nearly in pain from how hard and swollen I am, I imagine how all of this creamy stuff would be perfect for lubing up Raven's perfect, tight pussy. I grunt as the thought rushes in, and the lump at the base of my cock is already starting to swell up fat and round on both sides. I imagine shoving it inside her, locking her body to mine as I pump her full of—

My claws scrabble on the tile floor as my orgasm gets closer.

Claws? I open my eyes and find my legs are covered in thick fur, and my feet have shifted into huge paws. My hand is twice the size it was before and so is my cock.

Fuck. I duck my head so no one can see my ears over the top of the stall. I'm glad I'm alone in here because I'm not necessarily quiet when I transform. It only happens when my emotions are out of control, which usually isn't an issue at the office, not until Raven started doing that dripping-with-sex thing of hers, whatever it is. Now I'm sprawled out across the toilet, trying to stay invisible while I continue giving myself a hand job. I can't stop picturing Raven underneath me, her big breasts bouncing, her legs curling tight around my furry hips as I wedge my cock deep inside her. Ideally, she's coming around me as I reach my own orgasm, and I unload everything into her. Not a drop gets wasted as my knot seals her off, like a stopper in a dish drain.

Jesus. I'm thinking about *impregnating my coworker*. Fuck you, mating season.

My hand works faster, my claws scraping over my skin as I pump harder and harder. I'm strangling the damn thing imagining her sexy little phone voice making moans and mewls, and then my climax hits me like a ton of bricks to the head.

I can't help snarling as a burst of come shoots out of me. It's ejected with so much violence that it arcs through the air, painting the inside of the stall door white like a Jackson Pollock.

I sit there gasping as my body slowly returns to normal, then wipe the sweat from my forehead.

"You okay in there, man?" someone asks.

Oh, my god. There's been somebody else in here the whole time?

"Fine!" My voice pitches unnaturally high. "Just fine. Thanks."

After cleaning up the door, I yank my pants back on and try

to scurry out of the bathroom before my anonymous coworker can see me.

That woman is going to kill me, or make me accidentally reveal myself, which could potentially be worse.

RAVEN

I've been having strange dreams since I started using the vibe at work. Being a little bit turned on all the time must be messing with my brain chemistry, because this is the fifth night in a row I've dreamt about getting fucked by a huge, shadowy creature with the most divine dick I've ever felt in my life.

It feels so real that when I wake up, I'm surprised to find my pussy wet and shivering, almost on the edge of an orgasm. Damn. As if breaking up with Amos wasn't bad enough for my sex life, now I'm dreaming about giant cocks that would never exist in the real world. No guy could possibly compare to that.

The next day at work I'm distracted, and I screw up a few different times on customer calls. I accidentally reroute one to Connor's desk instead of the accounting department, because his extension just popped into my mind.

"Raven?" I hear him ask not minutes later. "Did you mean to send that account over to me?"

I sigh. I didn't bring the vibe today because I thought that maybe it would make the dreams go away, but that clearly hasn't made a difference in my ability to focus.

"Sorry, no." I scratch the back of my head in embarrassment. "I meant to send it to billing, but I got confused and pressed the wrong extension."

He arches an eyebrow. "The extensions aren't even close."

"I know!" I snap, and Connor leans back in surprise. "Sorry,"

I say immediately, awash with shame. I'm tired and I miss my vibe. "I haven't had enough coffee yet."

"That's okay." Connor is watching me with a concerned expression. "Is everything all right?"

It's a sweet question, but it's not like I'm going to tell him about the erotic dreams preventing me from getting a good night's rest. "I'm fine," I say quickly. I pick up my empty mug and tap the side. "I should deal with this crankiness problem, though."

He grins. "Of course. I know that I'm not human until at least cup number three."

I laugh as we leave the cubicle together. He pauses at his own as I walk by. "If you ever need to talk about anything," he says, "you can always come to me."

I blink a few times. I thought for sure Connor didn't like me after the other day, but now he's offering to bend an ear for me?

"Oh," I say, a little stupidly. "That's really nice of you. Thank you."

He just nods and sits back down at his desk chair, and he's almost comically too large for it. His long legs shoot out far underneath his desk.

Maybe he doesn't hate me after all, I think, as I go to refill my coffee in the break room. Maybe he's just shy. Or nervous.

Maybe it's the opposite of what I suspect, and he actually likes me. That would be a nice change of pace. I could certainly be interested in somebody like Connor, even if it's a little dangerous.

CONNOR

When Raven doesn't come in to work today smelling of her sweet, succulent arousal, I grow concerned. Yes, the break for my nervous system is welcome. I don't mind spending my day without a constant, raging hard-on. But I find that I miss it, too. I've gotten used to that glorious scent, which also drives me absolutely wild.

She seems off when I visit her cubicle, and I wonder if it's related. I overheard a few weeks ago that she broke up with her boyfriend. Maybe she's a little depressed.

At the end of the day, I'm surprised to find Raven standing outside the entrance to the building, leaning against the wall like she's waiting for something.

"Did your car break down?" I ask, stopping when I see her.

Maybe she isn't reeking of pure sex anymore, but all I have to do is look at her and it's like my nose can summon up the smell on its own. She looks simply delectable in the tight blue skirt and white dress shirt she wore today. They hug her plentiful hips, big tits, and round ass perfectly.

"No, my car's fine," she says, adjusting her purse nervously. "I was just waiting for you, actually."

Me? Why would she be standing outside the building waiting for me?

"What's up?" I ask. "Did you want to talk about the customer who called in—?"

"No," she interrupts. "I wanted to see if you, uh, would want to go out. Maybe. To get a drink? I would say coffee, but it's kind of late in the day for coffee, at least for me." She twists her shoe around, scraping the concrete.

Wait. She's asking me out. On a date. My mouth just kind of sits there, half-open, while I work through this in my brain.

Of course I want to go, that's not a question, if only just to keep smelling her up close and personal. Maybe I could even take her home and live out some of the little fantasies I've had about her. But going out with Raven is a terrible idea. Even if all that stuff actually happened and we got naked together, I couldn't just have sex with her. I would probably transform and try to mate her, and then everybody would be really upset.

"I'm not sure that's wise," I finally answer, hating the words as they come out of my mouth. Her big blue eyes lose their shine. "We're co-workers. We have to see each other every day."

"Right." Her gaze drops to her shoes and there's a tremble in her shoulders. "Of course. It was stupid of me to ask. I'm sorry."

Fuck. Maybe turning her down this way was an even worse idea. "You don't need to apologize—" I begin.

"I do. I just put you in a super awkward position without even thinking about it." She hikes up the strap of her purse and hurriedly pulls out her car keys. I don't want her to run. More than anything I don't want her to run. Her voice is shaky as she says, "Sorry again. I hope you have a good night, Connor."

Then she turns on her heel and darts away into the parking lot before I can even summon an answer.

Damn it.

RAVEN

I don't know what I was thinking. God, I was stupid. So, so stupid. Of course it wouldn't be smart to date my coworker. I just thought... It felt like he was trying to tell me something when he offered to talk. But he was just being friendly, and I read too much into it.

I go home that night and treat myself to delivery pizza and ice cream to help soothe my bruises. Then I head to my room and pull up some dirty artwork I've been saving.

I keep thinking about the shadow creature, the huge monster that I can hear snuffling and grunting as it plunges into me with that massive, incredible cock. I found my way to a forum just for people who have a kink for getting railed by big monsters and decided to check it out.

I found a wealth of what I was looking for and far more. It turns me on more than even my little bullet vibe. I lie on my bed with my laptop, dig out a bigger vibe, and lube myself up thinking of the creature in my dream. It's a great beast with pointed ears and yellow eyes that poke holes in the darkness. Somehow I feel like I know him, and I try to imagine that the thick dildo I'm pushing inside me belongs to him.

The next day at work, I put the bullet back in. At least I can feel good while avoiding Connor. That will take the sting out of getting rejected.

When I walk into the break room, of course he's there pouring creamer into his coffee. I say a quick "hello" and head to the other end of the room, pretending I'm here to get a fork, then scurry out as quickly as possible, even though what I really wanted was coffee. I can't face him after last night. Maybe I've already ruined our coworker relationship just by asking.

I spend the day turning up the power on the vibe, getting myself closer and closer to the finish line, only to slow it down again. Finally I can't take it anymore, and I head to the bathroom to finish myself off, running the vibe all over my clit until I finally break.

But my day doesn't get any better. The printer keeps jamming up, and it's all the way across the office in a creepy little room along with the scanner and the printer supplies. After the tenth time it jams, I run to the machine ready to tear it apart. I'm cursing at it as I open the panel to find the jam.

"You piece of shit," I growl at it, tearing at the paper. "Fucking worthless chunk of plastic."

"Raven?" I hear Connor say. "Are you okay?"

CONNOR

Holy shit. Today Raven smells like sunflowers and gold, like a good steak with a side of cinnamon roll. But she's shouting angrily at the printer, oblivious to the fact she's also radiating pure sex.

"What's going on?" I ask, stepping into the printer room. I was going to copy some signed paperwork, but now my nose is working overtime. The scent of her is everywhere, and it's starting to slip past my arguably meager defenses. I'm doing everything in my power just to keep my hands at my sides and not wrap them around her perfect hips. I could just push her up against the printer, pull up her skirt, and—

"The printer's jammed." She says it with such defeat in her voice, it's like she's just lost a war. "I can't get the damn thing to work, and I..." Raven trails off, then sniffles. "Sorry. I'm just frustrated."

I'm trying to stay in the moment, to help her with her problem and maybe ease some of her distress, but all my blood is flowing straight down to my groin. It's a very small room, with no windows and probably no vents.

"It's all right," I say. "Maybe I can help." I approach the printer and examine where she's half-pulled out the paper stuck inside. "I've had this happen before. You just need to reset the feeder. Hold on." I pry out the rest of the jammed paper, then open the drawer in the bottom. Raven peers over my shoulder as I work, and if my nose weren't already filled with the smell of her, it would be now.

I take out all the blank paper, tidy up the stack, and shove it back into the feeder. Then I press the little green button and we wait in silence as the printer sends the job through. Miraculously, it works and her document starts appearing in the tray.

Raven lets out a huge sigh. "Thank you. I've been fighting

this fucking thing all day and I was just about to go Office Space on it."

I chuckle. "No problem. Been there." Raven reaches for her papers. "Hey, Raven. I want you to know that—"

She holds up her hands. "It's okay. We don't need to talk about it."

But I do need to. I need her to know that it wasn't about her, or even about being coworkers.

As she rushes to leave the printer room, I grab her arm and she lets out a gasp of surprise.

"I would love to go out with you," I say, looking into her wide eyes. "More than anything. But you don't know about me. You don't know who I am."

I mean to say it menacingly, but she doesn't look afraid at all.

"You're Connor," she says, relaxing in my hold. "I know you're a good guy."

She has no idea. "I'm not," I growl. "I'm the opposite of a good guy. In fact, I'm dangerous. I could hurt you, Raven."

There. That will do it.

But then, she laughs. "Are you trying to scare me off?" she asks with a wry grin. "Because it's doing the opposite of that." She backs away from the printer and pushes the door behind her closed. Suddenly all that's left is the one fluorescent light overhead. I don't know what to make of her.

That should have made her turn tail, but now she just looks like she wants to eat me. Little does she know she's the one who will be devoured.

RAVEN

Connor moves lightning fast as he pins me against the printer. His pupils dilate until his brown eyes are all black, and his breath is coming hot and fast.

I barely have time to register that he's about to kiss me before his mouth seizes mine. It's no light peck, no exploratory first kiss. It's hungry and animal and already his tongue is laving over my lips, barging between them to explore even more of my mouth. Oh, god, does he feel good. This is how I want to be kissed. I want to be consumed.

I bury my fingers in his hair and pull him closer. The hands pinning me down start to slide roughly up and down my arms and chest and hips, pressing me harder against the printer. His hand brushes over my pocket, where I keep the remote control for the vibe.

Just a little pressure and the power is suddenly cranked up. I moan into Connor's mouth as the vibe goes nuts and his hips jerk against me. I can tell as he rubs against my thigh that he's grown thick and long down there, and it makes me shudder all over in warm anticipation.

His hands find their way under my ass and he hefts me up, and I'm surprised at his strength. Now I'm sitting on the printer and he's grinding himself between my thighs, never once releasing my mouth from his assault. My vibe is turning me into a shivering, moaning mess underneath him.

"Fuck," Connor groans, releasing my lips at last. He huffs against my forehead, his hands still gripping my cheeks and thighs. "I don't know how you're doing it, but god damn, you smell so good."

Smell? Huh. I didn't put on any perfume today.

Connor's grinding harder now, like he's trying to fuck me with our clothes on. I don't know what got into him but I like it.

No, I love it. He would be welcome to keep rubbing his body all over me if we weren't in the printer room at work. Hell, I'd probably let him fuck me right here.

"Connor," I finally manage. "Tonight. Can we finish this tonight?"

When I finally get a good look into his eyes, I find that they're bright yellow, like a wild animal's. I blink a few times, thinking I must have imagined it. But he quickly turns his head and grunts out a harsh, "Yes. Tonight."

He pulls away, and a surprisingly large package is tenting his slacks. I slide back down to my feet as he adjusts himself and takes a few deep, measured breaths.

"You can do this," Connor says to himself. Soon his boner has calmed down enough that he can look at me again. His eyes have returned to normal. Huh.

"Come to my house," he growls, his voice much lower and throatier than I remember it being. "I'll text you the address."

Then he pulls open the door and hastily walks from the room.

Is it just my imagination or do his arms look hairier? I've never paid that close attention before. But I'm absolutely thrilled for whatever tonight will hold.

CONNOR

She said yes. Oh my god, she said yes.

Oh, no. She said yes, which means she's coming to my house to finish what we started today in the printer room. Which means there's a good chance we'll take our clothes off, and once I have her naked in front of me, who knows what will happen?

I didn't really think this through. But god, I wanted nothing more today than to yank my pants down, scoot up her skirt, and plunge myself inside her. There was something driving her wild underneath me, making a high-pitched sound and sending sparks of her scent right up my nostrils. I must learn what it was.

I've been sitting in the dark for a while, just smoothing one hand down my leg where my cock is thick and hard under my jeans. I haven't been able to stop thinking about her since I got home. She said she'd be here in an hour, and I know that means she's taking a shower first, which I find disappointing. I loved how she smelled today, absolutely drenched in the scent of her sticky come. All I wanted was to lick it off of her.

That's all right. If I can keep my transformation under control, I'll still have my chance to make her gush all over and lick it up.

Big if.

Eventually I hear a car pull up outside, so I turn on all the lights. Don't want to look like a complete creep. There are footsteps on the front porch, and then, after a few seconds, a light knock at the door.

I take a few extra moments to answer just so I don't look like I've been standing there waiting. When I pull the door open, Raven is there in my entryway in the tastiest-looking outfit I've ever seen. A tiny spaghetti strap barely keeps her big, round tits in place, and I can even see the edges of her red bra at the low neckline. She wears high jeans over it, which hug her butt in the most shockingly hot and adorable way possible.

"Are you going to let me in? Or just look?" she asks tartly. I pull the door wide open and step to one side so she can enter.

"You look fucking hot," I finally say. The words are crude, but I can't think of anything else because she's occupying all my conscious thoughts.

"Why, thank you." She does a little curtsy with an invisible skirt. "You look good when you're not in your work clothes."

Does that mean I don't when I am? But by the lascivious smirk on her face, I don't think so.

Raven advances on me like a predator hunting for prey. She winds her arms around my neck and leans up, just brushing her lips over mine. I'm pleased to find we're going to dive back in where we left off in the printer room.

As if I've been picked up by a tornado, I'm sucked right into her. A second later I have her wedged as close against my body as humanly possible, one hand tangled in her hair, the other roving down her back and over the soft swell of her ass.

Oh, god, the smell of her. It's like nothing else on this earth. Every instinct in my body is going wild, screaming to rip off that cute, tiny spaghetti strap and everything else holding her body back from me.

"I didn't think you had it in you, Connor," Raven says as she pulls away to catch her breath. "You always struck me as the shy type."

If only she knew that it's a mask I carefully wear so I don't attract attention to myself. If only she knew I've been picturing her naked since March, imagining wrapping her around my cock and taking her against a wall. Frankly, all sorts of places, but not once did I dream that I'd be fucking her in my own house.

"You bring it out of me," I tell her instead, leading her into the living room by her hips. Here I can make her comfortable while I decide how best to go about this. I have to somehow keep my transformation under control, even though she'll certainly notice something is odd when she sees my cock, with its thick lump at the base.

"So I turn you on?" she asks with a wide grin as she slides down onto my couch. I follow her, making sure her head is comfortably propped on the arm before I start exploring her with my hands. I run them over her round tits, finding the nipples under her bra and teasing them with my thumbs. She wriggles underneath me, and, by the smell of her, she's already incredibly aroused. It pleases me immensely to know I'm the one doing it to her.

"Oh, you do turn me on," I murmur, kissing her neck, then her collar, as I play with her amazing boobs. "A great deal. I've been thinking about you for..." I trail off. Should I really confess to her how long I've been fantasizing about doing just this and more?

Don't mention your dream of pumping her full of your come so you can get her pregnant, my human brain warns me. Right. Normal human woman here.

"For?" she prompts, lifting her hips to rub them against mine. Oh, fuck. My cock is so hard already it might just burst through my jeans. Honestly, I wouldn't put that past it.

"Let's just say I've been thinking about it for a while." I return to her mouth and cover it with mine, sucking her lips, nibbling at them with my teeth. She groans and arches her back so her breasts press in the most tantalizing way against my chest.

Now I finally get to have her.

RAVEN

So he's been wanting me too, huh? That's an intriguing and rather pleasing thought.

Maybe I shouldn't have brought my vibe along on this trip, but I just couldn't help it. I wanted to be thoroughly turned on and dripping when I saw Connor, ready to get fucked hard. Hopefully he doesn't mind when he finds out.

But all this clothing is getting in the way of what I really want, so I head for my shirt and pull it up by the hem. Connor shifts backwards so he's straddling me, and I practically rip off the spaghetti strap. He lets out a heavy breath as my tits are exposed, barely restrained by my bra. This is the best one I had, and there are even matching panties under my jeans.

"Fuck," he grunts. His hand ducks under my back and unclips the band of my bra. I'm surprised at how vigorously he tears it off me, revealing my fat boobs and extremely hard nipples.

Without any preamble, he drops his head and starts to suck on them. Damn. His tongue makes a few laps around one of my nipples before he suddenly bites on it.

"Holy shit." It hurts, but also feels so damn good. He runs his tongue over the bite to soften the pain, and my whole body is responding. My pussy squeezes tight around the vibe, and I gasp in pleasure as he bites my other nipple. I'm whimpering and arching into his rough treatment. It reminds me of the shadow creature in the dream treating my body with as much ferocity as tenderness, fucking me deep while never once hurting me.

When he's done with my breasts, Connor kisses down my belly, stopping at the button of my jeans. He quickly pops it open and unzips them, and he climbs off me to slide them down my legs, taking my cute panties along for the ride. I realize then that my shoes are still on, and he pauses briefly to take them off, too. Suddenly I'm naked in front of him, and he's still wearing all his clothes.

Why is this so hot?

Before I realize what's going on, Connor has my thighs spread, and he's crouched down to drop his head between my legs.

Oh, my god. What guy goes right for cunnilingus? Connor, I guess. He's like a dream come true.

He runs his finger over my clit right away and I moan. Suddenly, he pauses.

"You're vibrating," he observes, one eyebrow arched. "Are you a robot?"

I giggle, then reach down between my legs. He watches curiously as I slide two fingers inside myself and withdraw the vibe, then turn it off with the remote.

His eyes go wide as saucers. "Oh. Wow." A sudden look of understanding comes over him. "So that's why you always smell like sex."

I blink. "What? You can *smell* me?"

It doesn't look like he meant to say that. Connor blubbers for a second. "Well, I, uh, you see..." He clears his throat, then quickly shoves his face between my legs and starts to lick me.

Every thought flies out of my head, and I drop the vibe to the floor by accident. He's attacking my clit with his tongue, sweeping back and forth over it in the most delectable way possible. I writhe and groan, and before long I find him sliding a finger in right where my vibe used to be. I'm definitely going to come all over his face like this.

"God damn," Connor mutters, pausing to breathe deeply. "You taste so fucking great."

Nobody's ever told me that in my life, and boy, do I like it. It only takes a few moments for my orgasm to spiral out from the place where he's tonguing me senseless and race up my spine. My back arches, and I let out a cry as it takes me over. Connor's still furiously licking, and before my last climax is over I crest a new one.

He groans against my pussy. "Fuck, yes. Come for me, Raven."

By the time he withdraws from between my legs I'm panting and twitching, every one of my nerves firing ripples of pleasure across my body. While I'm lying there pathetically, Connor sits up and yanks off his shirt. When I get a good look at his face, though, I find that again his eyes have changed color: they're bright yellow all over, like a wolf's. His arms are noticeably hairier, and, when he unveils his chest to me, it's shockingly hairy, too.

"Connor...?" I ask. What's happening to him? He's breathing hard, nostrils flared, and when he smiles down at me, his canines have grown significantly longer. Finally I ask, "Connor, are you a vampire?"

He pauses in the middle of unbuttoning his jeans to give me a strange look. "Huh?"

"Well, your eyes, and, um..." I point at his face. "Your fangs? You didn't have those before."

"Ah, fuck!" He gets up off the couch and rubs his face. "No, I'm not a vampire. God. No."

"Then what are you?" Unbidden, an image of the dark monster with the huge cock pops into my mind. It had yellow eyes just like his.

Connor's head is turned away from me, his dick trying desperately to escape his pants. His hands tense up into fists. "I'm not human," he says. "This is what I was trying to tell you. I'm not just some guy you work with."

Well, I gathered that much by now.

"Okay, but if you're not human that means you're something else." I sit up on the couch naked and reach for his arm. Whatever's going on, he's clearly embarrassed by it. Little does he know how much porn I've been hoarding starring many different inhuman things.

He stills under my hand, then finally looks down at me. His nose has begun to elongate, and fur is spreading across his skin. He's growing in size right in front of me, splitting all of his clothes wide open.

When Connor opens his mouth to speak, all of his teeth have become long and pointed. "Raven... I'm a werewolf."

CONNOR

Raven's blue eyes are wide as the transformation takes me over. I couldn't stop it, not after tasting her, not after slicking my hand in and out of her amazing, sopping-wet pussy, all prepared for me by that tiny vibe of hers.

God. That thing. So much makes sense to me now. Has she been wearing it every day at work? It's astonishing and really fucking hot. She'd be my perfect woman if it weren't for the fact she's about to go running from my house at full speed with no clothes on.

"Oh my god," she says, staring as my feet turn into huge paws with high hocks. My hands grow to the size of plates, long claws sprouting from the end of each finger. There's a *pop!* as my tail emerges from my spine, big and fluffy. Her mouth steadily falls open as I change, and by the time I'm finished, she's gaping at me. "So you are a werewolf."

She hasn't gotten up yet. Maybe she's just in shock, too stunned to move.

"Yup," I say, because there isn't much else to it.

"Huh." Raven still looks like she's seen a ghost, but now she's massaging her jaw as she closes it. Then she narrows her eyes suspiciously. "Wait. Are *you* the one who's been fucking me in my dreams?"

Now it's my turn to gape. Not only is she still here, still lying completely exposed on the couch to me... "What?" I'm dumbfounded. "What do you mean?"

"There's this big monster who's been, uh, visiting me at night. When I'm asleep."

I have no idea what to make of this, but it could explain why she hasn't taken off screaming yet. "I haven't been doing anything like that, I don't think," I answer truthfully. But the idea is stirring my cock again, and now it's starting to rise up in its full, transformed size. Her gaze travels down to it, and she gasps.

"That's it!" Raven sits up on the couch, transfixed. "I know that!"

Now I'm really confused. She's staring at my junk with the biggest smile on her face I've ever seen. "You know what?" I ask, almost tempted to cover myself up at the plainly lewd look she's giving me.

"It *is* you." There's powerful certainty in her voice. "You're the one I've been dreaming about for the last week. I would know that anywhere." She gestures at my throbbing erection. "It has that big round bit on the bottom."

My knot. She really does recognize it. Has my lust for her somehow manifested in her nightmares?

Curious, Raven edges towards me. "Can I touch it?" she asks, glancing up at me. She tilts her head as we lock gazes. "Man, those eyes are cool."

She wants to *touch* me? I'm starting to wonder if maybe I'm the one who's asleep. "S-sure," I manage. "Go for it."

When her hand wraps around my cock, I can't restrain my strangled moan. Encouraged, she strokes up the massive shaft, and pre-come starts to leak out. I haven't been touched like this in my werewolf form since I was rejected from the pack, and holy Satan on Earth, it feels amazing. Now that I'm changed, my nose is even more powerful than before, and the scent of her fresh climax is filling up every cavity in my head. I can't help growling as she reaches my knot, and massages it with her fingers. I think I might just go off right in her hand.

"Hold on," I grunt, pulling her away. Her tiny hand drowns in my big, furry one.

Raven looks worried. "Did I hurt you?"

I shake my head fervently. "No. But I'm afraid I'm going to

hurt you if you keep doing that." I want nothing in the world more than to pounce on her, push her down on the couch, and impale her on my cock.

"Hurt me?" she asks. "How?"

I can't help licking my chops. "By fucking you," I clarify. The longer I look at her, the longer I smell her, the more my animal urges are rising up into my conscious mind and taking over. Her little pussy is still dripping from when I licked her, and I think even if I'm a touch too big, she would be slick enough to stretch and fit me.

"Oh." She drops onto her back, head leaned on the arm of the couch once more. Delicately she reaches down to her swollen, pink folds, and starts to touch herself. "But that's what I want you to do," she says. "I've literally been dreaming about it."

This can't be real, can it?

RAVEN

Oh my god. Here he is, right in front of me—my dream beast. The shape of him makes a lot more sense now that I can see him in the full light. He's furry all over except for his chest, where his fairly muscular body has turned shockingly beefy. Just like in my dream, his cock is gigantic and has that lump at the bottom that I know will feel so, so good. His eyes are intense, and there's even drool gathering in his jaws.

Connor is literally my dreams come true.

"Come on, wolf guy," I say, curling one finger and beckoning him towards me. I want him inside me while I'm still fired up from that tongue-fucking session.

But instead of climbing on top of me as I expect him to,

Connor crouches down and slides his hands under me, picking me up as if I'm made of air. He carries me down the hall quickly, claws clicking on the wood floors, to a big bedroom with gray walls and black bedsheets. I like the feel of his soft fur under my bare skin, and I'm getting more excited by the moment for what's coming next.

When we reach the bed, he lies me down surprisingly gently, and takes a few heavy breaths.

"Raven," he says uncertainly. "I need to tell you. This isn't just a casual fuck. Not for me."

I arch an eyebrow. "I don't typically hook up with just any werewolf," I say with a chuckle, but he looks deadly serious.

"I'm looking for something more than that. If we do this—" He swallows hard. "—then I'm choosing you, and you're choosing me. I'm looking for a mate."

A mate? I wonder what that means to a werewolf. Is it like getting married?

It seems a little soon for that, but honestly, I'm game. Where else am I going to find a hot guy who turns into a monster?

"Okay," I say. "Then I choose you, if you choose me."

A wicked grin peels back his lips. "Oh, I chose a long time ago."

He hurriedly reaches into the bedside table for a plastic bottle, and his big clawed hands are shaking as he drizzles lube all over his cock, the thick veins up the side pulsing in time with his quick breath. Cock gleaming, he climbs onto the bed and grabs my thighs in his huge hands, dragging me towards him. His yellow eyes are piercing, and his lips curl in a growl.

Now I understand what he meant. His instincts are taking over, and he's going to fuck me hard and fast.

Perfect.

He grabs onto my nipples again with his mouth, and tongues them roughly as he guides his cock between my legs. The moment the head finds my chasm I know I'm going to have to stretch for him, just like I do in my dreams. Thankfully, he put the lube on thick, and my pussy easily parts for him.

"Fuck," Connor groans, his arms shivering where they're pressing down hard on the bed. "You're so tight, Raven." He's only got his head inside me, but already little sparks are spidering out from the place our bodies connect. His eyes are slammed shut, his black nose huffing great big breaths as he fights for control of himself.

"Connor." I reach up to stroke along his furry muzzle, and his eyes shoot open. "Just do it. Do it how you want."

His breath hitches, and then something else seems to take over him: the feral, raw creature that he's repressed deep inside. With a howl, he thrusts into me, and my entire body curls with the force of it.

"Oh god," I moan as that massive cock somehow, magically, fits inside me. Well, all of it except that big lump at the base. That hovers just outside me, as I'm not quite stretched enough to take it.

Not that this matters. Connor's got so much length that immediately I'm stuffed up to the brim. I can feel the head of him deeper than anyone's ever been, and I clench my legs tight around his hips as my body shifts to accommodate him. My feet brush the base of his tail and Connor jolts underneath me, and I wonder if that's a sensitive place.

"I can't believe it," he mutters to himself as he pulls his cock back out the way it went in. He groans loud and harsh as he shoves back into me, and it glides like a kid on a waterslide. I can't believe how monstrously good he feels widening me, pulling my layers apart until I'm so full there's no give at all in my pussy. I can barely flex my muscles down there, so I don't bother and let Connor take over.

His claws curl in the blankets, and I hear a *rip* as they tear through. He leans his head down to mine, plunging into me faster and harder, slicking in and out with slobbery noises.

Then his tongue is plying my lips apart, and once they're open for him, he jams it inside my mouth. It's long and thick and I moan as it tangles with my own. His mouth is wide open, his huge fangs leaking drool onto my face as he tongue-fucks me.

My tiny vibe has absolutely nothing on Connor.

"Raven," he growls, sitting back on his haunches and lifting me up by my hips to bury himself even deeper. "I'm going to fuck you so good and so hard."

Now that I'm wet and soft and open for him, I feel that lump at the base of him start to worm its way inside me. Oh, damn.

"Yes," I moan. "Please, please!"

I cry out as his lump slips past my entrance, stretching me even wider. I can barely hold my body together as he thrusts with more force, that ball-like knot slipping in and out, triggering bright explosions behind my eyes.

"You're mine." Connor's gaze is intense, those yellow eyes lasering into me. "My mate. All mine."

I nod rapidly as the head of his cock digs further into me, and the budding pleasure in my abdomen threatens to become a mountain. If I'm not careful, I'll topple right off the side.

"I'm all yours," I agree.

He snarls with satisfaction and drags his tongue down the side of my face. "And now," he whispers in my ear, his claws finding their way to my rock-hard nipples, "I'm going to pump you full of my come, and I'm going to keep doing it until you're fat with my cubs."

I nod my head furiously. If he fucks me like this every night, I'll happily become his breeding mare.

"Give it to me, Connor," I whisper.

With a moan of pleasure, he drags his tongue down my neck to the curve of my shoulder. I feel the tips of his teeth brush over my soft skin, and then suddenly, they pierce through.

I let out a scream as his fangs bury themselves in my flesh. The sharp pain of the bite is the last spark I need to reach for my climax. He roars and shoves through my tightening heat, and that's when I feel that lump starting to swell up. It rockets me over the edge and beyond, sending me even higher. It's as if the ceiling is crumbling as that massive knot fills and fills until suddenly, it can't move any longer.

"Your womb is mine," he grinds out between clamped teeth. Absently I can sense that I'm bleeding, but it only heightens my orgasm. Once more Connor plunges himself inside me, and then that huge lump fills so full it *sticks*.

I'm moaning, thrashing, pulling him in as deep with my heels as I possibly can. He groans as he hits his limit and suddenly, there's a hot burst right against my cervix. Somehow it feels painful and wonderful, and I can sense his gushing seed seeping through it. There are no more thrusts; there can't be with that massive lump jammed inside me. My cavern stretches and stretches to accommodate his load, and tears are streaming down my face as I'm pumped so obscenely full that I can't feel anything else.

"God! Connor!" He grips me hard, claws digging into the skin of my back as he pulls me roughly against his furry body. "Ah, fuck!"

"You're incredible," he whispers against my head. "Absolutely amazing, Raven."

We lie there, gasping and panting, as his claws finally loosen their hold on me. He draws them down my body, over my swollen belly as his breaths slow, and so do mine. But that huge cock of his is still stoppering me up, and my abdomen aches while pleasure continues coursing through my bloodstream.

Finally, I feel the blood drain out of him, and his cock is almost violently ejected by my strained, tight pussy. Come spurts out, drenching my ass and the bed underneath me.

Connor doesn't seem to care and collapses on top of me, just barely avoiding crushing me with one arm. He licks the wound on my shoulder, drawing the blood away.

"What was that, by the way?" I ask.

"Oh, sorry. It's just instinct. Now if you ever come across another werewolf, they'll know you're mine."

That's kind of neat.

He sniffles across my face with his cool, wet nose. "God damn," he groans. "You're amazing, Raven."

I'm still too out of breath to answer, so I just bury my face in his furry neck. Once we're a little more recovered, Connor scoops me up with one arm and rolls me into his chest.

"Did you mean all that?" I finally ask. "All that stuff you said about like, getting me pregnant?"

After a beat, he slowly nods.

"Yeah. I did."

I smile against his thick pectorals. Little baby werewolves sounds like my kind of crazy. "Cool."

CONNOR

What did I do to deserve a woman like this?

I finally pull out, and my instincts know exactly what to do. I get between her legs and clean her up with my long tongue, making sure to soothe the raw, red edges of her sweet pussy. Then I bundle her up tight in my arms, curling my haunches underneath her so she's fully encased in me. I smooth her hair down with one hand and rub over her sore belly, which is still full of me.

For the first time, the urge to mate has abated. I feel at peace in a way I've never felt before and it's intoxicating. My tail wags behind me, content and happy for the first time in years, as we fall asleep.

We're both late to work the next day. It was just too impossible to drag ourselves out of bed. My werewolf form has been satisfied, so it lies quietly inside me when I wake up to the overpowering scent of sex. I fuck Raven again anyway, though I know my human cock doesn't quite live up to my transformed one.

We start going steady after that. I take her on a "first date," and she dresses up in the hottest little green number I've ever seen. To my surprise, the wolf wakes up again, and that night I take her hard from behind, the way I've always craved. I fuck her until she's screaming and then shoot everything inside her again, relishing the way her ass quivers with the force of her orgasm. My knot jams itself inside her again, making sure none of my potency can escape.

Raven's pregnant only a few weeks later. Without much pomp or circumstance, she packs up her apartment and moves into my house, where I can dote on her every moment like she deserves. We let the office know that we're not only dating but getting married soon, and everyone is a little shocked.

Sheepishly, I reach out to my mom, who still lives with the pack, to let her know I have a cub on the way. She's surprised.

"You managed to find a human willing to be your mate?" she asks over the phone, amazed.

"She's pretty special, Mom."

And she is. My Raven, my blue-eyed queen, takes up every last corner of my heart. Well, all of them except the spot reserved for the growing cub in her belly.

"Will she be a werewolf, too?" she asks, groaning a little as she adjusts her big, swollen body on the couch.

I shrug. "Maybe, maybe not. It's a gene like any other."

"Huh." She leans against my shoulder. "That will be a fun little surprise someday."

After Mom advocates for me, Raven, and our new baby, I'm welcomed back into the pack. Somehow, Raven fits in smoothly with them. Maybe they all share a little of the same crazy. Eventually, it's like I never left at all.

My wild, perfect woman. All mine.

The Last Dryad

MESHISAWATAKI. THAT'S HIS NAME. "BUT TAKI IS FINE," HE SAYS, ears drooping a little. "That's what everyone calls me."

We're not allowed to give out their names to the guests on our tours. While I'm walking around the park introducing each of our resident monsters, explaining their diets and their behaviors, I refer to them by what they are: Demon. Merman. Centaur. I talk about them like they're exotic animals in a zoo, and with every surprising new fact ("Did you know Merpeople have a fully polyamorous society?" or "Dryads are strictly vegetarian.") everyone on the tour *oohs* and *ahhs*. I hate dehumanizing the residents this way, but it's my job, and I make a livable wage in exchange.

It's generous of Taki to make conversation with me on a cloudy day like today when there aren't many people visiting. I'm not popular with most of the monsters at the Menagerie—understandably so.

"But your full name is so pretty," I tell him. "I like it."

He perks up again, and a little smile dances at the edge of his mouth. "Thank you." I've always enjoyed how musical his voice sounds when he's pleased. "I don't think anyone's said that to me in a few hundred years."

Right. Dryads live a long time—forever, if they have everything they need and don't meet an untimely end at the barrel of a hunter's gun. Unfortunately, since humanity has done such a thorough job of destroying the dryads' natural habitat, that's not the case anymore.

I'm sitting on a bench next to his exhibition wall, twisted around so I can look through the plexiglass. His voice is a little muffled, but I can still hear him. Every once in a while he leans too far forward and his antlers tap the surface, making him cringe.

Finally, I ask the question I've been meaning to ask every time we sit down and talk together on my lunch breaks.

"What happened?" I ask. "Why did you come here, where there aren't any trees?" Sure, the decorators have put in a whole host of indoor plants and even some fake evergreens inside his apartment, but it's not the real thing.

"There was nowhere left to go," Taki says. "Someone cleared the wooded area where I was living to plant a vineyard. I can't pay rent. So I was fined for trespassing, and that was it." Taki's eternally cheerful attitude doesn't match the story he's telling me, but I've gotten used to that. Somehow he's always so pleasant, so optimistic, even though he's lost so much. "When I got to the city, everybody was staring at me. I didn't know what to do. Then I met a very kind manticore who gave me a card for this place." He looks around at the little habitat they built for him in the Menagerie. "It's the best I could ask for, I think."

He has such low standards. You would think we'd protect monsters and their natural habitats given how rare they are now. The spotted owl has more legal protections than Taki does. Instead, people expect them to get jobs and live normal lives, as if they could. Who would employ a four-hundred-year-old forest nymph with mossy legs and antlers? It's not like he can wear pants or shoes with haunches like his. Technically he's always naked, but the word doesn't really apply to him. You can't see anything at his crotch—it's all hidden under the leaves that grow naturally out of his body.

The Menagerie is the perfect place for someone like Taki to land. He's taken care of here, in exchange for a little show-and-tell with tourists.

"What will happen to you living away from nature?" I ask. It must be awful for him not to be in the forest where he belongs.

"I will die, eventually," he says, and again his upbeat manner undercuts his sad words.

"That's horrible!" I can't believe humankind would do this to him. "You need to get out of here."

Taki smiles at me with an unfathomable gentleness. "This is the best place for me, Ana. I'll still get a long, happy life here. It just won't be forever."

"Happy" doesn't sound right at all for a forest creature forced to live behind a plexiglass wall. Surely a peaceful, kind being like him deserves better. But it's not as if I have anything else to offer him, or suggestions for how he could possibly return to the wild in a world where every inch of land is owned by *somebody*.

"You look worried," Taki says, frowning. "I think I've upset you."

"No, no. It's not you." I shake my head and sigh. "It's us. I hate that humanity has done this to you."

Again he smiles, and it's a warm, affectionate one. "Thank you for being so concerned for me. But it was not a malicious thing. Humanity simply moved on, grew, and changed, while some of us didn't. I'm an artifact."

A beautiful one, I think. Taki has a slender nose, a sturdy chin, and high, distinctive cheekbones. He reminds of an elf from *Lord of the Rings*, with his long ears and perfect dark hair that falls straight and shiny around his face. His bare chest is muscled but sleek, his shoulders broad but not huge.

It all seems very unfair that he should be trapped here.

That night, I have my weekly phone call with Mom. She likes to check in on me as often as possible. I'm an only child, and since Dad died she's directed all of her attention and affection toward me. I don't mind it, though, since she doesn't hassle or nag me. She just needs someone to talk to.

"How's the job going, honey?" she asks, same as she does every time we talk.

I give her the usual "It's fine" line and prepare to move the conversation on to my roommate's latest drama, or the novel her book club just read. But I haven't been able to stop thinking about Taki since our conversation the other day so it comes out of my mouth without me realizing what I'm saying.

"Actually, there's this dryad at work," I tell her. "One of the residents."

"Oh?" The tone of her voice has changed to indicate she's keenly listening now. She loves any tidbits I drop for her about the Menagerie and comes on my tour every time she visits. "What about him?"

I suddenly feel quite flustered, not sure why I opened this door. But I proceed to explain the story that Taki gave me about how he ended up there, and Mom *tsks* at the proper places.

"Terrible," she says. "He sounds like a very nice young man."

"He's a dryad, not a man. And he's like four hundred years old, Mom."

"But he looks young, doesn't he? I seem to remember seeing him last time I visited." It's true that Taki doesn't look a day over twenty-five, even though it seems there are more lines under his eyes now than when I first started this job. "He must miss the great outdoors so much living in just that little apartment."

"It's not really like they organize field trips, either," I say. "Sometimes everybody goes to the Safeway on a bus for snacks and that's about it."

"That's so sad," Mom says.

All I can do is agree. I can't change Taki's situation, not unless I had a whole nature preserve of my own to give him.

Suddenly, Mom shrieks on the other end of the line.

"What? What is it?" I'm clutching my chest, hoping my heart is still inside it.

"The cabin!" Mom starts talking at top speed. "Remember how dad's parents had that cabin up in the mountains? We took you there all the time growing up. It's on twenty acres or so, isn't it?"

"Wait, Mom." I can't understand everything she's saying. "That place is still around?"

"Sure it is. Grandma and Grandpa didn't take that good of care of it in their later years, but it's still there. We pay the property taxes."

I wonder what kind of shape it's in now after all this time. Does the plumbing still work? What about the heating?

Twenty acres. That's nothing to sneeze at. Maybe it's not the woodland paradise where Taki spent most of his life, but it's secluded, and the other plots of land out there are just as big and mostly unoccupied.

"Ana?" Mom asks at my silence.

"Yeah, I'm here. Just thinking. Are you suggesting I take him out there?" I don't know if they'll even let me. Then again, Taki is a voluntary resident. He's not a prisoner, so he can leave anytime he wants. He just chooses not to. Not like he has a car, though.

But I have a car. I wonder if his antlers will fit in my little hatchback.

"That is what I'm suggesting." A speck of mischief creeps into Mom's voice. "Go out there on one of your weekends with him. Let him enjoy nature again. Your dad's parents didn't develop it at all, not past that little garden they used to have."

She's right. It could be perfect, if Taki is even interested.

"Thanks, Mom. I'll ask him and see what he says."

I get a thoughtful little *hmm* in return. "If you do go, have fun, dear."

It's a few days before things calm down enough at work that I can have a private conversation with Taki again. I've been trying to think about how best to float the idea so it doesn't sound like I'm trying to kidnap him.

Finally there comes a day when one of my tours is cancelled thanks to the rain. Holding an umbrella, I sit down at the bench in front of Taki's exhibition room, getting the underside of my jeans soaking wet.

"Ana," he says, smiling widely when he sees me. "It's good to have your company again." He puts down the knitting needles he's holding.

"What are you making?" I ask. I didn't know he had taken up knitting, but then again, there probably isn't much for a captive dryad to do in a modern world.

"Not sure. A blanket, I suppose. Is that too ordinary?"

I have to giggle a little. "I think that's a great place to start. Everyone likes blankets." Time to broach the subject. "Hey, Taki?"

He cocks his head. "Yes? Do you have something on your mind?"

"What if you could go out and be in nature again? Just for a day or two? Would that help you?"

His eyebrows go up. "I do miss the trees," he says thought-

134

fully. "The ivy. The soft forest floor under my feet. But where would I go? I don't have any means of transportation."

"Let's say you did. And let's say there were twenty acres of land with nothing on it but woods. Would you want to go?"

Now he's studying me with interest. "What do you have in mind, Ana? You seem to be formulating a plan."

He sees right through me, of course. "Look, my mom reminded me that my grandparents had a cabin out in the mountains, about a three-hour drive from here. We still own it. There's nobody out there, and it would just be you and the forest. I could take you up there on my weekend, if you want."

His dark green eyes are surprised at first, then they crinkle with pleasure. "This is a very generous offer," he says. "But I wouldn't want to put you out. You would have to drive me there and bring me back again only two days later."

I shrug. "Not like I'm doing much else." I don't have a boyfriend, and my roommate is kind of a drag. My friend group is small and mostly made up of introverts. It would be nice to get away. Besides, there's a not-so-insignificant part of me that wants to spend some alone time with Taki and maybe, just maybe, get to know him a little better. He's beautiful and preposterously kind, and I feel like he deserves to have everything.

"If you truly mean that," Taki begins uncertainly, "then I would be delighted to accept. But..." His face drops. "I don't know if management will allow it. Any sort of relationships between us and staff members are strictly prohibited."

He sounds like he's read the rule book, even though I'm pretty sure he can't read. You don't do a lot of book learning living alone in the woods for centuries.

I hadn't considered that angle. We were warned early on not to make friends with the residents. But Taki is a free agent —he should be able to do what he likes with whoever he likes, right?

"I'm sure I can convince them." Dana, the staff manager, will see that what I'm offering is harmless. She's a pretty decent boss. "Just wait here, okay? I'll talk to someone."

Taki gives me a wan smile, like he doesn't share my hope. That's the first glimpse I get that maybe the dryad isn't showing me his full self yet.

"Thank you, Ana," he says. "Know that I won't be disappointed, and I'll always value your friendship."

It sounds like a breakup text. But I shrug it off and give him a thumbs-up, then head off to ask my boss.

Taki's antlers do manage to squeeze inside my little hatchback, but it's a tight fit. He can't move his head all that well unless he sits just so, and he's going to have to hold that position for the whole three hour drive each way.

"Are you sure this will work?" I ask, starting up the car. "You're going to get a crick in your neck."

"What is a 'crick'?" he asks, slouching his shoulders slightly to ease up the pressure on his horns. "My neck will be fine. My body is much more resistant to pain and fatigue than yours."

It took a little ass-kissing and sweet-talking to get Dana—and then by extension, her own boss—to agree to let me drive Taki out to the woods. But I argued the point that as a dryad, he *needs* the trees. Already he's showing signs of age living inside that apartment. Dana agreed that he was a resident with special requirements, and they couldn't very well import a forest for him.

Besides, it's better for the Menagerie's bottom line if their resident dryad lives longer.

So her boss's boss reluctantly wrote me a three-day pass to take Taki out to the cabin for the weekend, and had me sign a half-dozen forms to clear it.

Already my heart is fluttering high in my throat as we head out of town, into the farmland. Taki is strangely quiet, staring out the windows as we pass fields full of hay bales and big irrigation systems.

"This was all forest," he says after a while. His voice sounds far away. "Most of what you see here."

"How do you know?" I wonder if dryads have magic powers. Some monsters do, even though the scientific community debates as to whether it's a placebo effect or not.

Taki sticks a hand out through the open window, and gasps in surprise as the wind blows it backwards. "I can feel them," he tells me, testing the air a second time. He starts to anticipate the wind, and curls his hand into a fin so he can cut through the air, the way a little boy would. "Their presence is still here, their roots holding the earth down. Their ghosts will always inhabit this land."

"Wow." I can't imagine what it's like to feel so much. I don't have to be tormented everywhere I go by the memory of a place that no longer exists. "I'm sorry."

"Why are you sorry?" In his rush to turn his head towards me, Taki bumps his antlers on the ceiling of the car with a grunt.

"Humans like me did this. We cut down all those trees to grow feed for cattle."

His smile is gentle. "None of this falls on your shoulders, Ana."

I like how kind the words sound, but they don't make me feel better.

We talk of less serious things as the car winds up into the hills, then hills grow into mountains. Then, finally, we're there.

Nostalgia sweeps through me as the car comes to a gravelly stop in the dirt driveway outside the two-story cabin. There was just enough room here for my grandparents, my parents, and me whenever we did a trip. The kitchen was cramped, but that was fine when I spent most of my time outside anyway, running through the trees and reveling in my freedom.

I'd almost forgotten how much I loved visiting here as a kid until we step out of the car, and I'm hit by fresh, cool air and the familiar scent of pine trees. My lungs inhale it all in, feeling new and clean.

"Oh wow," I say. "It's beautiful out here."

But Taki hasn't said anything yet. He's simply standing there, arms held out to either side of him, head tilted up to the sky. I get the sense that something is happening, even if I can't see it, so I hold my breath and wait. After a moment, he turns to me, and all the grey under his eyes has vanished. He looks young and spry and his cheeks are full with color.

"Ana." It comes out a breathy whisper. "Thank you. Thank you for bringing me here."

I swat him gently on the arm. "Stop. We literally just got here. You can't thank me for anything yet."

"But I want to." He takes my outstretched hand in his, and squeezes it. His eyes are soft—so damn soft—as he looks at me. "It means a great deal to me that you would go out of your way to bring me here."

God. I must be blushing like a spilled can of tomato sauce. He releases my hand and I use it to rub my cheek surreptitiously. "Seriously, no big deal. I'm going to just unload. If you want to, you know, go out there..." I gesture into the woods. "Go on ahead. I know it's been a long time."

Taki tilts his head curiously. "Go on ahead?" he echoes. "What do you mean? I'll help you unload."

"Well, we came out here so you could go frolic through the forest, right?" I wave him off again. "So go. I brought some books and stuff to entertain myself."

A look of hurt crosses his face. "You had not intended to spend the weekend together?" His voice is heartbreaking.

Aw, fuck. I just want to cradle his cheeks in my hands and

assure him I want nothing more than to spend the weekend with him. But wasn't the whole point of this trip so he could have his "return to nature" moment? He doesn't need me for that. He probably wants the time alone, if anything.

"It's not that," I say. I pull one of the bags out of the trunk. "I just thought you'd want to enjoy your time in nature. Run wild with your hair blowing in the wind or whatever."

His expression morphs into one of pleasure. "There will be plenty of time for that," he murmurs. "Let me assist in unpacking and making a meal."

I blink. "You can cook?"

Taki laughs at my expression and takes the bag in my hand. "Yes, I can cook. I prefer to make my own meals because I don't eat meat."

I hold up one of the bags of groceries, which is full to bursting with produce, then start repeating my line from the tour: "The dryad is a strict vegetarian. You wouldn't eat one of your forest friends, would you?"

I'm surprised when Taki laughs, a sound bigger than his usual quiet chuckle. "Every guide has a different line, but I like yours best."

I've always thought the monsters found us annoying with our little canned jokes.

"But that's not why we don't eat meat," Taki continues. "It's not why I don't, anyway." Together we carry the bags inside.

"It's just a joke. I never even thought about it, honestly. But why don't you eat meat, then?"

Taki sticks out his tongue. "It disgusts me. I just hate the taste, honestly."

After I locate the key under a rock, the front door of the cabin opens with a heavy creak. It's warm inside, and has a faintly musty smell. Even with the lights on, everything is surprisingly dim.

As soon as I get the groceries unpacked, Taki locates a knife and starts cutting up the vegetables. I'm riveted to his hands while he slices everything just so. It had been my plan to cook for him, but he takes over the reins without even asking, and soon there are vegetables searing in a pan and he's making up some kind of thin pancake bread to eat it with. There's still a full pantry here, with all the dry goods inside big plastic containers so mice and bugs can't get in.

"Your grandparents had a very nice home," Taki says as we sit down to eat. I feel as if I've been carried along in his whirlpool this whole time, and now there's a nice, hot meal sitting in front of me, like magic.

"Oh. Thank you." There's still a neat layer of dust on everything, unfortunately. "It's all my grandparents' doing. They liked to come out here on weekends, too, and when I was a kid we'd come and visit them in the summer."

"I like learning more about where you're from." His eyes are just so *green*, and right now they're the brightest I've ever seen them. Why do I feel like he's seeing through me? I get another little shiver in my belly.

"Would you like to go for a walk?" Taki asks. It's so strange to see him in this place that has so many memories for me, half covered in moss and leaves, the other of half of him bare, perfect skin. It's like bringing a wild animal into your living room. "Ana? What do you say to a walk, together?"

My eyes snap up to his. Right. He was asking me a question that I definitely know the answer to. "Yes, please. I'd like that."

But we're only a few yards into the trees when I realize just how dark it is out here without the ever-present glow of city lights. Reflexively I grab onto Taki's arm, and he chuckles.

"Don't worry," he says. "Your eyes will adjust."

"Can you see in the dark?" I ask.

"I can navigate, if that's what you mean. The trees and plants tell me where they are."

So not only can he feel their presence, but he can talk to them, too? You learn something new every day.

Before too long my vision is taking in more and more of the shadowed trees and hidden shrubs, just like he said. As much as I don't want to, I finally let go of Taki's arm as we wade deeper into the forest. But his hand doesn't leave the place where it's ever-so-lightly touching my body. It feels like he's electrified, and his fingers are sending little shocks up my spine.

The air is thicker between us as we continue on our walk, and his hand falls back to his side. His step grows lighter the farther we get into the woods. Soon we hear the ghostly babble of a creek up ahead, and when we reach the edge, Taki crouches down to run his hand through the cold water.

"It's so fresh and pure up here," he says with wonder. "A marvelous place, truly."

"I'm so glad you like it. It's nice to see you happy."

He turns to me and smiles radiantly. "It helps to have such good company."

I thought I must be a burden for him, wandering through the dark like a lost lamb. "You're sure you don't want to be alone for a while? Talk to the trees and stuff?"

Taki turns so he's facing me, and then most unexpectedly, takes a step closer. He peers down at me, some of his dark hair escaping from behind his antlers.

"No." With a slow, quiet ease, he brings a hand up to my cheek. It's so intimate and gentle that my heart freezes up. "I don't want anything but to be here, enjoying this place with you." He strokes a thumb over my cheekbone. "I can't figure you out, though."

I'm mystified by that. "There's not much to figure out." I'm pretty simple, overall, being a tour guide at a home for monsters with a mostly unused English degree.

"Oh, there is much to learn about you, Ana." Taki's tone has dropped an octave, and his dark eyelashes fall low over his eyes. "You keep insisting that I don't want you here, when you're the reason I came along on this trip in the first place."

That can't be right. He wanted to be out in the forest, out in nature, to reclaim his connection to it. The act of being here has clearly made a difference already. His smooth skin is shining in the moonlight, and the leaves that cover his body from the waist down ripple in the breeze. But I can't explain why he's looking at me as if none of that matters.

"Me?" My voice comes out a little too high pitched and squeaky. "You came because of me?"

Silently his thumb drops to the edge of my lips and they part of their own accord. What is he doing? I search his eyes for some sign, but all I see there is a growing heat, steady and hungry. Does he want me as much as I've been wanting him?

Taki leans down towards me, and that's when I realize his answer. He's seeking me, asking for permission to take a step further. And I will happily take the leap with him.

I open my mouth and draw my tongue over the pad of his thumb, and the gasp Taki lets out is delicious. He traces my lip, spreading my saliva along it until it's smooth and slick. Somehow his touch went from sweet and innocent to completely erotic in a single breath, and it's making every last blood vessel in my abdomen pulse. I bring his thumb into my mouth, circling it with my tongue, and his green eyes close with pleasure. His other hand falls to my waist, his fingers sinking into my flesh under my shirt as he pulls me closer. With our hips almost touching I can feel his leaves grazing my belly, and my breath sticks in my throat. I don't know what we're doing, or what Taki's body entails underneath the greenery, but I'm interested in finding out.

When I release his thumb, his eyes open again and they're the same dark, deep green as the trees around us. I don't have to ask him to know what he's thinking because I'm thinking the same thing. I reach up to push some of his long hair back behind his pointed ear, the one now standing at full alert. Both of his arms are brushing up and down my back, hinting at what could be an embrace if I want it.

Do I ever. I lean into him, face tilted up so I can look into his, and this time his smile is mischievous. I knew he had another side.

"I want to kiss you, Ana," he says, drawing a line with his hand from my lower back to my hair, showing me with feather touches what else he'd like to be doing. "And much more than that, if you're willing."

This beautiful man—dryad, I suppose—is offering himself up to me? I'm more than willing.

Instead of answering I kiss him first, and immediately he sweeps me up so I'm pressed tight to his chest. I gasp into his mouth and he devours it, dragging his fingernails up and down my hips. Suddenly Taki is ravenous, traversing every inch of me with those lovely hands while his mouth sinks into mine. His tongue is eager and his teeth pluck at my lips, making me ache in the most delicious way.

That's when I feel it against my thigh, and I break away from our battlefield of kisses to look. The leaves have parted, revealing a cock darker than the rest of Taki's skin. The shape is strange, long and segmented halfway up with another layer of skin, and it has a firm head pointed down rather than up.

A tremor runs down my belly, between my legs. I want to know what it feels like. What does he plan to do with it?

"Ana." Taki's voice is husky and soft in my ear. "I've wanted you since you first sat down on that bench and spoke to me."

I shiver under the sensation of his breath on my neck. "I didn't realize," I say. "I... I want you too, Meshisawataki."

At the sound of his full name, Taki groans. He kisses my ear, then my jaw, then my throat as his hunger spills through. His cock swells even further, rising upward to press insistently at my belly. Now that it's out there—now that we both know what the other wants—I'm eager to have more. I need more, so I reach down and gently take him in my hands.

Taki buries his face in my neck, his grip tightening around me as I stroke up, then down, then up again. When I reach the head, there's slippery pre-come sliding out the tiny slit at the front. Rubbing it around to lubricate my fingers, I continue pumping him, relishing the sensation of each of his foreskins moving back and forth. He grunts and his hips buck, and he sucks on my neck in a way that will surely leave a hickey later.

"Wait." He gently wraps his hands around mine, drawing me away from his cock. "I want to touch you. Please."

Before I even send a conscious command to them, my fingers are unbuttoning my jeans and pulling them down my thighs, where they get stuck on my shoes. Taki slides a hand down my belly, under the band of my underwear, seeking out the warm place between my legs like a heat-seeking missile. I gasp as his cool fingers meet my wet, swollen folds, and he chuckles into my ear.

"You're so soft down here." His gentle voice caresses me. "And so ready. Ready so soon." He nibbles the shell of my ear.

"Yes," I whimper. "I'm ready."

But Taki just shakes his head and leans back, so he can look in my eyes. His fingers slowly pry me open, and then he slides one from my hyper-sensitive clit down to the wet slit below it. "I was going to take this slow," he says, that playful look returning to his face as he slips a finger inside me, "but I'm not sure that you want that."

No, I don't. We're out in the middle of the woods, for god's sake, and there's no one else around for miles. I know exactly what I want.

"I want to feel you. Show me how you fit inside me."

There's a rumble low in his chest, something I haven't heard before. He presses his mouth hard against mine, sucking on my lips, fucking my tongue, all while he dances around my clit.

Then, suddenly, he pulls away. "Turn around." The command takes me by surprise from someone as demure as Taki. He withdraws his wet fingers, and brings them down to stroke his cock. There's a thirst in his eyes that's new, that thrills me. I do as I'm told, and my entire lower half is shivering with the knowledge of what's going to come next. Then I bend forward and place my hands on the tree, exposing myself to him as much as I can given that my jeans are still around my ankles.

"Ah," Taki groans. I watch over my shoulder as he rounds on me from behind, and his fingers return to my most sensitive place. He teases my nub, while something larger, something wider and firmer, presses into my small opening.

"Oh, god." It's been months since I had sex with anyone, and I'm tighter than I'd hoped. Not to mention that his cock is bigger than any human's. The head sinks in, and I gasp and drop my forehead to the tree bark.

There's no way he's going to fit.

Hands find their way under my shirt, running up my back and then down again, over my hips and my ass in a slow, comforting gesture. As Taki's hands stroke me, he pushes in just a little more, then a little more still, and my tight muscles start to give way underneath him.

Oh, does he feel good. Better than good, like thick silk. I'm relaxing for him, softening for him, as he tests each depth and settles into it, hands still roving over my skin. When I glance at him over my shoulder his eyes are intent on mine, his hips almost flush with my ass. I can't fathom how he fit all of that into me, but now I'm fuller than I've ever been, and that mouth-watering pointed head is pressing against something sweet and taut deep down inside me.

I moan when he pulls back again, withdrawing almost all

the way. I feel his hand reach underneath us, teasing my clit, spreading my juices around my swollen lips.

"You are so wet and hot and tight, dear Ana." He leans forward, and slides all the way back in. It feels like nothing else. My back arches up into his belly, and his hand travels to my breasts where they still hide under my shirt. I didn't read anywhere about dryads being incredible lovers.

His thrusts gradually speed up, and now his hand is tangled in my hair, holding me in position firmly as he owns me. Every time his hips connect with mine I feel his leaves glance over my clit, over the soft flesh of my ass, and I'm starting to swell up like a balloon. Soon, if he keeps up that agonizing, perfect pace, digging deep inside me for treasure, he's going to find it.

"Taki!" The cry that comes out of me echoes in the trees. "Faster, please!"

The sound he lets out is almost a roar, and that's when I feel him starting to change. He's growing inside me, and suddenly I'm full, so full, and he's towering over me. When I turn my head I find him taller, his antlers sprouted bigger and broader, leaves and vines winding up his body and toward mine. One vine wraps around my thigh, holding me in place as he moves again, spreading me wider than I ever thought I could possibly go.

"Oh, god!" I gasp as he pulls himself out.

"Sing for me," Taki murmurs, and I barely recognize his voice. It booms over me. "I'm going to take you until you scream my name."

When he sinks all the way in again, I cry out and grip the bark of the tree. The vines are winding under my shirt, tearing it open, freeing my breasts from the bondage of my bra. Taki's huge hand suddenly lands next to mine as he falls forward, and there's a wood-like texture to his skin. His other arm explores underneath me, from my clit up to my nipples, rubbing and plucking and tantalizing them until I'm shivering. My knees are getting weak now, but Taki's huge new body is holding me up as he pounds himself into me. Every thrust fills the balloon bigger and bigger, until I'm so tight that I can hear squishing with every thrust.

"Yes," he whispers, running his hand over my belly and pressing me even closer, even tighter against him, making us even more deeply connected. "Just like that, Ana."

Fuck. His girth is stimulating every single nerve ending inside me, and the balloon is ready to burst. I scream, and I think it's his name, but it's so tangled up with my gasps and pants that even I can't tell. My cries drive him even harder, and soon he's plundering me for all that I'm worth.

That's when the balloon pops.

"Taki!" The sound comes out strangled as I crumple forward, and Taki's arms catch me. He roars as I clench tight around him, sending blitz after blitz of immeasurable pleasure through me, and he plunges deep one last time.

There he stays, nestled in my squeezing, rippling channel, and I feel like the bones have been sucked out of my body. His hot come fills me up, slipping out around us and dribbling to the forest floor.

Still buried inside me, Taki pulls me into one strong arm and supports us against the tree with his elbow. There are bits of bark wedged in my palms, but I can't even feel them. My body is just a husk filled with bliss.

Taki has returned to his normal size, and eventually he slips out of me. I can somewhat hold myself up now, so I reach down to pull up my pants and button them back on. I know they'll be soaked wet between the legs by the time we get back.

"I'm sorry about your shirt," Taki says as he helps me unwind some of his vines from my thighs.

"That's okay. It's not like anyone's going to see me out here."

"No one except me." He grins a wolfish grin, and I think I've seen the other side of him tonight. We walk back to the house together, hand-in-hand.

"You can't like, get me pregnant or anything, right?" I ask as we approach the cabin.

Taki laughs. "No, I don't believe we are compatible."

"So... you need lady dryads to make, uh, dryad babies?"

"Hmm. I suppose so. But there aren't any left."

I pause at the doorway to the cabin. "How many of you are there?"

He shrugs. "I don't know. It might just be me."

But he doesn't seem bothered by this, as if he knows his time on this world has already ended and he's become a relic of an age long past.

When he fucks me on my childhood bed that night, he is gentler and sweeter, and doesn't become the monstrous creature that took me out in the woods.

But he will again when we go for a hike tomorrow.

THANK YOU FOR READING!

If you enjoyed this book, please consider leaving a review! Written reviews help authors like me reach new readers.

Join My Newsletter!

For all the latest regarding books, and to get access to lots of great free content, sign up for my newsletter!

www.LyonneRiley.com

Also by Lyonne Riley

TROLLKIN LOVERS

Stealing the Troll's Heart

Healing the Orc's Heart

Capturing the Orc's Heart

Tempting the Ogre's Heart

TALES OF MONSTROUS ROMANCE

Prince of Beasts

About the Author

I come from a traditional publishing background, which is rewarding but often too rigid, so I shifted to self-publishing to pursue my real passion in writing: extremely sexy monster romance. I probably should have known I would end up here after spending most of my young adulthood writing erotic fan fiction, but it took me a while to find my way back to myself.

Acknowledgments

I would like to thank everyone involved in helping me through the process of putting out this book. I can't say enough how much I appreciate the help and encouragement of the people around me—especially Amber, who told me I could do this in the first place.

Huge thank you to Rowan Woodcock for the beautiful cover illustration. And to my critique partners, especially Ruth, who give me phenomenal editorial feedback: You all make this possible. And of course, my amazing spouse, who has always supported my dreams—and given me lots of inspiration for my characters' sexy adventures.

I couldn't have done this without the expertise of my fellow self-published romance authors. Thank you for inviting me into your circles and helping me through this process.

And thank you to my readers, who gave this book a shot.

Made in the USA
Monee, IL
14 November 2023

46502500R00100